Clearing

Clearing

Iris Wolff

Translated by Ruth Martin
Edited by Monique Charlesworth

MOTH
BOOKS

First published in German as
Lichtungen by Klett Cotta Verlag in 2024

Moth Books Ltd, PO BOX 80244, London W9 4LN

Published in English by Moth Books 2026

This edition published by arrangement with
Gaeb & Eggers Literary Agency

Manufacturer: York Publishing Services Ltd
64 Hallfield Road, Layerthorpe, York YO31 7ZQ
Tel: 01904 431213 | Email: enquiries@yps-publishing.co.uk
Website: www.yps-publishing.co.uk

Represented by: Authorised Rep Compliance Ltd.
Ground Floor, 71 Lower Baggot Street, Dublin D02 P593, Ireland
www.arccompliance.com

ISBN 978-1-917593-04-5
ISBN 978-1-917593-05-2 (eBook)

Edited by Monique Charlesworth
Typeset by Clare Brayshaw
Cover design by Dan Jones

GOETHE
INSTITUT

The translation of this book was supported by a grant
from the Goethe-Institut

For my mother and Mane

AWARDS

Clearing was shortlisted for the German Book Prize in 2024 and that year won the Uwe Johnson Prize.

In 2023, Iris Wolff was awarded the Chamisso Prize, Hellerau, and in 2024 the Spycher Prize Leuk.

In 2025, she received the Konrad Adenauer Foundation Literature Prize, one of Germany's most prestigious prizes, honouring writers who 'give freedom a voice'.

'Iris Wolff's *Clearing* succeeds in deeply embedding her two protagonists within the European history of the late 20th century. Both - like the author - originate from Transylvania in Romania ... With great sensitivity and narrative sophistication, this coming-of-age story is told in reverse, tracing how their paths in life fractured, while anchoring the characters in specific spaces and landscapes.'

Jury nomination, German Book Prize 2024

'Like Johnson, her narratives reconstruct a world that has gone. In so doing, she shows us how historical events disturb and disrupt the lives of individuals. *Clearing* also explores, in literary terms, what home can be, or is. And, like Uwe Johnson, Iris Wolff refuses to supply a moral along with the story. That is left to the reader.'

Jury decision, awarding the Uwe Johnson Prize, 2024 for outstanding literary works relating to German history, past or present

'With poetic elegance and in dense, vivid scenes, Iris Wolff shows how freedom is lived. Against the horrors of 20th century ideology, her novels preserve humanity and show a deep commitment to values. She portrays lives scarred by European history, those from diverse languages and religions who question belonging. Her novels (*Blurred* and *Clearing*) are beacons of light in contemporary history and make a pioneering contribution to the European culture of remembrance.'

Jury decision, awarding the Konrad Adenauer Foundation Literary Prize, 2025

PRAISE FOR CLEARING

'Highly original – a wonderful novel to remember, dream about and ponder'

Die Zeit Book of the Month

'Iris Wolff tells her stories through images that linger and remain in the mind: life in rural villages, in family chronicles, clandestine meetings shadowed by secrets and oppression; forest clearings that yet are places of inexpressible hope. These images are enriched through exact observation, by patient listening; they inspire fascinating associations, which is what great literature does.

Helmut Sturm, *Literaturkritik.de*

'In my view, her novel is also the best of the six - indeed the best of the twenty nominated for the German Book Prize.

Denis Scheck, *SWR Kultur*

'All that is essential in Lev and Kato's relationship lies behind and between their words – just as it does in Iris Wolff's literary universe as a whole. In *Clearing*, short sentences across fewer than 300 pages create a world that contains everything. Wonderful, truthful, and highly recommended!'

Katrin Kaiser, *Abendzeitung*

'The artistic device through which the characters' present actions become clear only as we learn more of their back story, vividly illustrates Kierkegaard's insight that life must be lived forwards but can only be understood backwards.'

Stefan Kister, *Stuttgarter Zeitung*

'Scene by scene, Wolff carefully conveys her information, telling [...] of the unbreakable relationship between Lev and Kato. [...] She does this in a prose that is restrained and quiet, precise, poetic, and simply beautiful, with a melancholy undertone.'

Gerrit Bartels, *Tagesspiegel*

'*Clearing* is more than just another novel about Romania by Iris Wolff. It is the psychological portrait of a soul wounded by different forms of dictatorship, surviving because it is able to wait and, in the end, [...] managing to shake off the most merciless dictatorship of all: the sense of not being enough for another person. [...] A magnificently contemporary book."

Andreas Platthaus, *FAZ*

'Iris Wolff tells of friendship and love poetically, of life in today's Romania for those who decide to stay in spite of everything, and for those who seek their happiness in the West. A great read that rightly made the shortlist for the German Book Prize.'

Annika Depping, *Bücherstadt Magazin*

‘With great confidence, Iris Wolff lays bare the deeper layers of a fragile relationship, as the story unfolds step by step in reverse.’

Oliver vom Hove, *Die Furche*

‘Reading *Clearing* is a great, and sometimes dizzying experience that lightly upturns all the supposedly self-evident expectations of literature and storytelling, and simply makes the reader happy.’

Irmgard Hölscher, *KommBuch*

‘We are dealing here with an extraordinary novel, one that addresses an impressive cornucopia of themes within the smallest space.Most fascinating of all: nothing in this book stands in isolation; everything is connected.’

Tomas Gärtner, *Dresdner Neueste Nachrichten*

‘Wolff tells the story of Lev and Kato […] with great sensitivity and poetic imagery, weaving the history of an entire country through their conflicts and family entanglements. As soon as you reach the end, you want to read again from the beginning, to do justice to all facets of this novel.’

Babina Cathomen, *Kulturtipp*

‘In her understated style, Wolff once again proves herself, in this fifth novel, to be a master of impressionistic realism.’

Gérard Otremba, *Rolling Stone*

'The colours and nuances are what make *Clearing* such an experience: a novel that emphasizes diversity, tells its story gently, poses questions, and leaves the judging to the readers. It doesn't confuse identity with belonging, and thus values both the becoming and the being of its protagonists. […] A wonderful European portrait.'

Michael Kuhl, *Kuhle Bücher*

'*Clearing is* a novel in a minor key that by no means shies away from the horrors of Romania's past.'

Carsten Otte, *tazInes*

'Iris Wolff has mastered the art of omission, and she also equips her characters with this ability. Some things are deliberately left unsaid; some take years to be spoken. […] In this novel, she questions how friendships grow - becoming more intimate as friends seek their own paths, whether together or independently.'

Claudia Ingenhoven, *mdr Kultur*

'Through its reverse storytelling, *Clearing* unfolds its very special narrative appeal […] we encounter Kato and Lev not as literary figures […], but as people we might happen to meet somewhere, whom we gradually learn more about. And it's just what they themselves are willing to tell. That is what is so special about this truly fabulous novel.'

Marie Kaiser, *rbb*

'For those who don't yet know: in Iris Wolff we have a special literary phenomenon!'

Anton Thuswaldner, *Salzburger Nachrichte*

'In her highly poetic novel, Iris Wolff tells a timeless love story that goes journeying into the past, to arrive, almost by chance, squarely in the present. Many regions in Eastern Europe today are shaped by those who have left, as entire generations of young people have moved west. In *Clearing*, Iris Wolff portrays them in literature of great beauty and elegance.'

Jürgen Abel, *Literatur in Hamburg*

'Unreal in its substance, and how complete it is.'

Gerrit Bartels, *rbb Kultur*

'It [the book] is very sophisticated and yet - that's the wonderful thing - it is completely natural, completely light.'

Iris Radisch, *Die Zeit Podcast*

'A truly outstanding book in many respects: political, but not intrusively so [...] A deeply poetic and uplifting book: intelligent and linguistically [...] very convincing.'

Anne-Dore Krohn, *rbb Kultur*

'Her old-masterly yet light tone, her use of leitmotifs and gaps, her ability to make important, meaningful details light up - there is something magically compelling here.'

Julia Schröder, *SWR 2*

'With extraordinary, powerful, and tender images, Iris Wolff tells of childhood and youth in a dictatorship where repression grows like mildew on people's souls, paralysing them into tolerance. If language could dance, this novel would be a duet of yearning lovers swirling in pirouettes and leaps.'

Annemarie Stoltenberg, *NDR*

'She narrates Lev's story from the present back into the past, as he lives through the political and social events in Eastern Europe, and does this intensely, with an incomparable feel for atmosphere varying from austerity to opulent sensuality.'

Julie August, *Bücherschau*

'A quiet and intelligent novel about leaving and arriving. [...] With fine strokes and muted colours, she paints a world in transition."

Holger Heimann, *WDR 3*

'She stays close to her characters, whom she describes with loving precision, in a gentle language that is as exact as it is poetic, both intense and cautious, never sentimental or accusatory."

Christiane Schwalbe, *Neue Buchtipps*

'Iris Wolff handles her narrative with confidence. Her story lies between speech and silence, between the factual and what is intuited, between past and present.'

Carsten Hueck, *Deutschlandfunk*

'*Clearing* is a melancholy, quiet book; once again, Iris Wolff weaves a calm text, rich with images. [...] Iris Wolff has succeeded in combining personal stories and contemporary history both convincingly and enchantingly.'

Petra Reich, *LiteraturReich*

'With the certainty of a sleepwalker, Iris Wolff trusts to her minimal style, one that gives respect and dignity to even the minor characters. [...] She never departs from that steady narrative voice, one which never slips into kitsch yet evokes what remains unspoken between the lines.'

Rainer Moritz, *NZZ*

'With great devotion, Iris Wolff's new novel tells of timeless friendship and how the opening of European borders has changed relationships.'

Susanne Schramm, *Aachener Zeitung*

'Wolff's language captures the spaces between people; love, friendship or distance chime to the rhythm of her sentences.'

Cornelia Geissler, *Berliner Zeitung*

'Wolff's novel could easily be described using such general terms as 'identity' or 'influence', but the heart of this book lies not in theses, but fine details and the way minimal differences are captured in language and transformed into images.'

SWR 2

'Wolff is a master of impressionistic realism, who captivates her readership in a melancholy, gentle, poetic, and pointed way. A magnificent novel about the choice to leave or stay in times of social upheaval.'

Gérard Otremba, *Sounds & Books*

'Against the backdrop of political upheavals in Eastern Europe, Iris Wolff's clear precise imagery describes the power of strong bonds, and the experience of being a foreigner at home inside a fractured society.'

SRF

'The way in which she spends pages describing the death of a tomcat or the songs of blackbirds, bringing trees into focus, or evoking sounds, is unparalleled. Iris Wolff has found a very distinctive narrative voice that is sober and rich in detail, yet never drops to mere realism of detail. In the most natural way, social and political happenings are constantly peering in through the window and into private life.'

Cornelius Hell, *ORF Ö1*

PRAISE FOR BLURRED

Nominated for the 2026 Dublin Literary Award

'Mediated smoothly by Ruth Martin in translation, Iris Wolff proves to be a superlative storyteller. Shuttling between several temporal planes, combining lyrical passages with precise, almost clinical descriptions, and navigating between striking flashbacks and digressions of all kinds, she is a master of the teasingly slow dramatic build-up. The result is memorable prose, subtle and mesmerizing.'

Costica Bradatan, *The Times Literary Supplement*

'A memorable, brisk and enaging evocation of the blurred lines of border, language and generation'

Bryn Stole, *The Berliner*

'This novel, with the breadth of an epic and the lighteness of touch of a fairytale, is a pocket history of 20th-century Romania. […] All in all, the lives in this book are presented "so vividly you think you remember them yourself".'

John Self, *The Guardian*

'These lives are delicately and intimately drawn; sometimes tragic, though never melodramatic. Blurred is elliptical and allusive, yet limpid. It engages the reader using brushstroke moments of clarity and feeling.'

Rónán Hession, *The Irish Times*

Book of the Year

'Skilfully translated from the German by Ruth Martin. Ingeniously constructed, and largely set in rural Transylvania [. . .] seven apparently discrete and wonderfully evocative stories gradually coalesce into a gripping and moving novel about a young man coming of age during the Ceausescu period.'

Peter Parker, *The Spectator, Books of the Year*

CONTENTS

Sas pe thai nas pe.

Nine

The ferry trailed a frothing line of foam. A white arc in the blue, marking their course long after they had passed. The smell of diesel, loudspeaker announcements hacked up by a wind so strong they could lean into it, shirts inflated, trousers flapping as it roared in their ears, heads, bodies. They could still feel that roar minutes later inside the ferry, an aftershock, an echo, and Lev couldn't help thinking of stopped saw blades continuing to vibrate in a wilful, humming rhythm, the floor suddenly still, the sawdust that hovered over the machine falling with a slight delay, startled by gravity.

Cold air streamed out of air conditioning units, grasping hands, ankles, paper, the stones and shells sitting in their pockets like washed-up flotsam. Kato wrapped a shawl around her shoulders, pulled up her legs. Lev turned a pinecone in his hands; it came from the tree in whose shade they had eaten lunch. With swift, questing strokes Kato sketched a girl who had fallen asleep on the seat opposite. She had documented every day of their trip, capturing scenes they had observed or experienced, and sometimes Lev himself: a man with a long beard, unusual for him, reading in a café, at a newspaper kiosk, leaning on the car, roadmap in hand.

Lev sought her gaze, but it was snagged between girl and sketchbook. The charcoal stick blackened paper, fingers and the heel of her hand. She turned a page, started again. It was impossible to disturb her when she was so absorbed.

Under the pine tree, he'd said he had to go back.

Kato didn't seem angry or surprised; she responded calmly, as if she'd guessed what was on his mind. And maybe she, too, wanted to pick up her familiar routine again, return to her life. But in what city, what country? This trip was a departure for him, a new beginning, but for her it was a transition, maybe even a conclusion. And yet in these opposing movements they had found one another again.

They'd been travelling for six weeks, from Zurich to Paris, then Nantes, Montpellier and east along the coast. They had drifted, sometimes spending whole days apart; they didn't need many words for their moods, their ideas. They knew each other too well; they'd been apart too long. They looked around towns and villages, went walking, swimming, while the beaches emptied with the approach of autumn. They behaved as if time didn't exist, just the endless space of the road ahead. And for a while, that's how it was, he wasn't deceiving himself. What lay between yesterday and tomorrow was gossamer-fine. And then his thoughts began turning to home more often: a sense of worry and longing was calling him back, but he said nothing, waiting for the right moment, which didn't come.

You always had to be ready to set off, said Kato, without looking up from her drawing.

'Even if you've only just arrived?'

'Especially then.'

Kato put the drawing of the girl in her folder.

She hadn't worked on their trip, had created only one picture in Paris, on the street outside the Louvre. For all those who didn't get to see the original Mona Lisa.

Outside the windows, the coast was approaching, docks, breakwaters, boats, the palm-fringed promenade. The tall houses painted in different colours, with their hundreds of eyes and window shutters. Streetlamps came on, their flickering light spreading over the hills. It seemed windy on the mainland.

Then everything happened very quickly.

'I'm coming with you,' said Kato.

Busy putting the water bottle and pine cone into his bag, Lev paused, so surprised he almost forgot to breathe. Kato's look was amused and slightly mocking. Impatience took hold inside the ferry, passengers packing their things and thronging the exits. The roller door rattled down over the kiosk. The girl was woken and walked to the stairs holding her mother's hand; her smile brushed Kato in passing.

'We're going back together?' he said, to make certain, when they'd reached the Land Rover on the vehicle deck. It had taken him that long to find his words.

He didn't want to be happy too soon.

He didn't want to lose her again.

'Yes,' said Kato. Just yes.

For the moment, that was enough.

Jestem znakiem podróży.

Nieruchomym.

Eight

'Excuse me.'

Lev came to a halt.

People jostled him, looked him up and down; everyone was in motion, hurrying, driven on at the same brisk pace. He had joined this stream, been swept along the carriage and the platform where the trains were standing ready to depart, where passengers were waiting, expectant, self-absorbed. He'd stopped in the high-ceilinged concourse, loudspeaker announcements, footsteps, voices, rumble of suitcases, all vanishing into the immense height. Then he spotted the large clock, set off again and turned right into the passageway towards the fountain. The street noise grew louder, car horns, engines; the rumbling and rushing ebbed as people dispersed across the square and, finally, he could stand in peace and look around.

Before him lay a road with several lanes, a zebra crossing, rows of five-storey buildings; blue and white trams pulled up, and the slip of paper in his hand told him the tram number, the direction, the stop. He compared the routes with his notes, didn't trust his judgement, looked at all the signs again. Found one more stop, further down the road into the city. The sense of relief was short-lived; at the ticket machine, the back of his neck grew hot, and he felt dizzy looking at the boxes, buttons, tariffs, coin slots, delete button – did he have to put money in, or press something first? Uncertain, he tapped a few buttons, then someone asked him a question. Lev stepped aside and let the man pay, trying to see how it was done, but by the time it was his turn, the tram was there. People got on, and for a moment he considered joining them, but how shameful to be caught without a ticket. A sense of futility came over him, as if this was the last tram and he had missed his chance.

The tram moved off with a crackle that scuttered ahead of it down the rails. Lev stayed at the stop, put down his holdall and turned the note over in his hands as if something yet to be discovered was written there. A woman was plaiting her waist-length, red-blonde hair; a man watched open-mouthed from a bench. Pigeons took wing, flew across the street, lined up along the parapet of a building. Something startled them into flight again. They were dark grey with white undersides.

Lev watched them wheel through the air.

From light to dark. From dark to light.

Something made him turn around. She might have been observing him for a while, might not have known what to say to him, wanting to be alone for a while with her recognition – that's what he would have wanted. To stand still, not saying a word, looking at her: her pale eyes, the line of three moles on her cheek, her gaze defiant, distant, aloof.

She had always triumphed at this game. She could hold your gaze longer, was never the first to break off a hug, to give that little signal, the hint of withdrawal that makes two bodies part again. Lev didn't have long for this first, quick examination; he took in her features, her posture, noticed what had changed and what had not, surprised by the magnitude of his joy, his excitement, and relief – for the old bitterness was gone.

She was wearing jeans, trainers and a green top, no jacket, despite the evening chill. A large bag hung from her shoulder. She seemed thinner but also more muscular, as far as he could tell; her hair was shoulder-length and still undecided whether to be straight or curly. He looked at her hands, the sharp bones of her wrists, the paint under her fingernails.

Some things were new, some unchanged.

'What are you doing here?'

'I had this feeling,' said Kato.

She bought him a weekly travelcard from the machine. They rode several stops on the tram – Kato said *Tram* like the locals did, not *Straßenbahn* – and the streets seemed to stretch on forever, with their tall, well cared-for buildings, their rows of shops and cafés. He started to feel he was straying, losing himself; his attention was all on her, her voice, her presence, the way she navigated the city and spoke German as if it was only natural, and although he'd had the whole train journey to imagine this moment, it had slipped from his grasp – he hadn't known what it would be like to see her again after five years.

Kato took him to a bed and breakfast, paid for a week upfront despite Lev's protests (she won over the woman behind the reception desk in a matter of seconds), counting out the notes onto the desk, and he decided not to work out what the francs were in lei, it was too depressing. He ran a hand over the wood, thought: maple, felt the rounded corners. The woman told him when breakfast was, when to vacate the room on departure day, what hours the reception was staffed, slowly, as if he was hard of understanding, and then quite casually squashed a moth that had settled on the desk.

Kato suggested dinner, but he pleaded tiredness. They said goodbye with a hug and he was the first to pull away.

His room was on the second floor. He opened the wardrobe doors, looked in the drawers of the table, tested the mattress, flicked lights on and off, stepped out onto the balcony. Then he unpacked his bag, took a long shower and got into bed.

Headlights swept across the ceiling. Through the open window came the crackle of trams; a couple was chatting on the next balcony. The city felt strange in its sprawl, its order and moderation, and he tried to reassure himself with the thought that the same laws applied both here and there. There is time, he told himself, there is a language that is yours, too, and no one will throw you out for not belonging. Especially – and the thought made him smile – not now you have a weekly travelcard.

Kato had sent him postcards from every country she and Tom had travelled through, her slanting handwriting filling the blank space. When she reached the bottom, she kept writing around the edges, making him turn the cards clockwise, once, twice before reaching her signature. Sometimes the cards were just drawings: urban canyons, statues in fountains, flowers, trees, a lot of portrait studies. And then, four weeks ago, the card from Zurich with the sentence, 'When are you coming?'

Just four words and a question mark.

He had read the sentence over and over. Had it matured over time, or been written on a whim? Did she mean the immediate or the distant future? Did the question signify that she needed or missed him? Did 'coming' mean to visit or to stay? Or was it not even meant, but just the kind of thing you might say to call up a particular, comforting feeling?

The phone call to arrange a time and place had not been the moment to ask. As they never spoke on the phone, their conversation was purely an exchange of necessary information. Then he waited for her to hang up, but no click came, and he pictured her in the stale, warm air of the phone booth, ear to the receiver, head resting on the glass, listening for him to hang up – which he then did.

One thousand five hundred kilometres to the east, the summer was dry and dusty. But here the lake cooled the city, made it bearable. The Paradeplatz was a shady, busy public square. Lev checked the city map that Kato had annotated, bore left and came to the Münsterhof. Someone was playing the accordion; a table was being carried out of an antique store. Lev held the door that one of the men had pushed open with his back, then carried on towards the river.

The rush of water, bells, footsteps. Kato's voice.

Which was always a little deeper than expected.

She was by the bridge; canvas, chalk boxes and a few loose chalks were scattered on the pavement. He gave the picture on the ground, overwhelmingly large and detailed, no more than a fleeting glance. Right now, everything else seemed more important. Her chalky hands, her posture, crouching, facing the picture and yet half upright; she'd had this care, this commitment, this concentrated absence while creating a picture from the very beginning.

She thanked everyone who threw something into the basket.

He wanted to keep watching, but she noticed him. The concentration vanished from her face and gave way to a smile, a surprised smile, a hint of how unlikely his presence here was. She stood up, wiping her hands on her trousers and, without thinking too much about it, he hugged her. Her skin was warm, with a scent he didn't recognise.

The trolley she used to transport her equipment to the pitch every day stood by the bridge parapet. The day before, she had told him that she no longer drew on the pavement but laid down canvases with pre-drawn outlines. Passers-by only gave money once they could see some colour.

Lev leaned on the parapet a short distance away. An older lady in a pale summer coat stopped to chat with Kato as if continuing an earlier conversation. At lunchtime, a man in a suit and tie gave her a sandwich. Kato clearly knew the workers who spent their breaks by the river, the children walking home from school, the homeless people who slept in parks. She preferred to listen to music, she said, but for the most part tried to stay approachable; the conversations were part of it. She earned money from her street art, so much that she had opened an account and put some away. Now and then, someone would commission a picture, and sometimes restaurants asked her to do some interior decoration. She worked every day. Only when it rained did she visit museums, to find new images to recreate.

Kato leaned beside him, held out half the sandwich.

'Do you always make pictures here?' he asked.

She had no choice in the pitch she was allocated, Kato explained; the permit for a spot had to be applied for by the week, sometimes by the day. 'But let's just say that I get on with the lady in the office who allocates them.'

'And the passers-by,' he added.

It was like living in a shop window, Kato said. Then again, this was the biggest gallery you could imagine. On some days she made very little progress because people wanted to talk, to unburden themselves of their life stories. Some offered to do her laundry; others chased her away. She was one of the travellers, the stranded, the ones other pedestrians mostly didn't see or didn't want to see.

After just a few hours of watching, Lev had an idea of what she meant. Folk hurried to work or to the shops, met in parks and cafés, while outside their front door, their workplace, in the streets of their city, there existed an unknown world of people who were there for a time and then gone, without any announcement or explanation.

That afternoon he went for a walk, to internalise the city's topography. You couldn't do that in a car or on public transport. This was a city of water, of sheltering green spaces, of benches and grand buildings, a city that was new, unwritten, with no memories lurking around its corners. And yet: a lot of things were coming closer here.

He walked into a supermarket, down the aisles. With a dozen versions of every product to choose from he took his time deciding, picking things up, putting them back, going for the cheapest one. He didn't like these huge, functional shops; they had them in his country now, and people went rushing around in pretend nonchalance as if to erase the shortages of earlier times.

Every corner here held an excess of life, shops, cafés and restaurants where people met to talk, drink coffee, stave off boredom. He surrendered to the city's pulse, its size, but every time he said anything, the words felt heavy and dull in his mouth. His origins were in his accent, they were sewn into his clothes and shoes.

A family was waiting outside an ice-cream parlour, clearly tourists; the two girls looked listless, passive. Lev knew the arrogance that comes solely from being young.

Someone had left a book on a bench.

A woman burst into tears, and no one comforted her.

Clouds gathered; the street darkened.

In the dark, it was easier to overcome the distance between belonging and foreignness, remembering and forgetting.

Over dinner, Kato said she didn't know what she would do at the end of summer. She liked travelling, but she also longed for some new purpose. You got used to a place, made friends, inevitably you left something behind. Then she paused, perhaps realising that applied to Lev too – the leaving behind.

'Where were you happiest?'

'In Rome,' she said. 'The whole city makes you want to

paint. And here. I like the clarity and the open spaces. In a way, the city holds me, it makes me feel secure.' She looked at him while saying this, as if adding something to the sentence in her mind.

It had been hard, she said, especially in the beginning. After just a few months she swapped Sigi's bike for a new one, a smoother ride. 'Don't tell him,' she'd written, and Lev had not; to this day, Sigi was still informing people that she was travelling the world on his bike.

Lev knew that she and Tom took breaks in the winter months, that Kato had delivered advertising leaflets in Slovenia, waitressed in Italy, worked in a department store in Germany. She now told him that they had bought a car, because they were tired of sleeping in a tent, and because despite their best efforts their belongings had multiplied; boxes of things had been left with people they knew in almost every country they'd been to. Kato had had to learn a lot: how to travel when money was tight; where you could wash; that a particular kind of politeness kept others at arm's length.

She wanted to know everything: how his mother and siblings were doing, what news from their friends Imre and Milena, how his visit to his grandfather in Vienna had gone. Lev tried to keep the tone light and wondered why she was avoiding certain topics, why she said nothing about Tom, why she didn't tell him what those four words meant.

He told her about the changes in the sawmill, his eldest brother gaining a senior position in the church, his younger brother moving his family to Cluj-Napoca, his sister wanting to divorce her husband, the different paths his niece and nephews were taking. He told her about Imre and Milena's wedding, the bridge that collapsed and still hadn't been rebuilt, and the new shop in the village.

Something about the way Kato reacted to this news, superior, knowing, angered him. She had no idea; she was judging the world he described from memory, as if things never changed, as if the village was stuck inside a glass snow globe where an occasional little flurry might be whirled up, but nothing worth mentioning ever happened.

Everything was different; everything had changed.

The glass was gone.

On his way to Zurich, Lev had stopped off at his grandfather's. Ferry and his wife lived in Vienna's Fourth District. Café Goldegg was his study and living room, where he ate his meals, read the paper, played chess, and where he'd met his wife, Krista. Even nearing eighty Ferry was an attractive man; his hair was shoulder-length, he still smoked with a cigarette holder, and spoke with that aloofness that sometimes came across as intellectual, and sometimes as arrogant.

Krista picked Lev up from the station.

He asked how she'd recognised him.

'You look like him,' she said, but he didn't think so. With his freckles and reddish-brown hair, he didn't look like anyone in his family.

His Romanian grandmother had always said that Lev looked like his late father, while Ferry claimed him for his own line – and Lev had never liked it when either side tried to co-opt him. He refused to be cast as German or Romanian.

Some people put a hyphen between the words, but that didn't feel consistent with his family history. His mother was a Transylvanian Saxon and his father Romanian; his grandfather invoked Austrian ancestors. Lev, a mixture of all this, didn't feel obliged to class himself as anything.

Ferry was sitting on a green banquette by the window, wearing a white shirt and grey checked waistcoat. He laid the newspaper aside and looked as if he couldn't quite place who was standing before him. It was only when, from behind the marble table, he announced to all and sundry that this was his grandson that Lev realised how flustered his grandfather was, how delighted to see him again.

He would love to show him Vienna, Ferry said over dessert (vanilla cream slices and coffee with whipped cream): St Stephen's Cathedral, the Naschmarkt, the imperial palace, the West End, Café Prückel, everything – the cafés, the shops, the museums, the people.

Did those four types into which his grandfather divided humanity exist in Vienna, too? In Ferry's opinion there were only saints and lunatics, clever people and idiots. Regrettably the lunatic was becoming ever more commonplace and the idiot more acceptable in polite society, so these days you hardly knew who was which.

Next time he would stay longer, Lev promised. He meant it, and yet he knew how improbable this sounded. He could have come to Vienna long before, but over the years he too had acquired something of Ferry's reticence and distance. Ferry had come to visit only twice since the revolution, once when the borders opened, to pick up the things he had left at his daughter's house, and then one summer he'd brought Krista to show her where he was born. Ferry couldn't understand why his daughter Lis didn't emigrate, why any of the Germans in Romania chose to stay after decades of being fenced in. In Ferry's opinion, their time was over – from a nation to a national minority to a… what?

'But you've found your place here, haven't you?'

'Certainly have,' said Ferry with a sideways glance at his wife. 'Once you go, you're always someone who goes.'

They finished the evening with a glass of port on the balcony, a tiny ledge you could go out onto from the kitchen, though going out was an overstatement; the backs of their chairs were still in the room. Krista had already bidden them goodnight. Her footfall could be heard in the flat for a while, and then it was quiet. Ferry smoked in silence, his feet up on the railing. Lev did likewise.

'Are you well?' Ferry hesitated and then nodded towards the railing. 'How are the legs?'

Lev closed his eyes, listening to the sounds of the rear courtyard. From open balcony doors and windows came the clatter of crockery, muffled voices.

'They do what I need them to.'

He didn't say that a kind of numbness still took hold whenever he thought about the accident.

'I never blamed you,' said Lev. He had no idea where these words had come from; they must have been inside him a long time, waiting for the moment when he was able, and obliged, to say them out loud. He'd withheld them from his grandfather long enough. All of a sudden, Lev felt light. Behind this lightness lay something else, a hunch or supposition, something he couldn't quite grasp.

'Your mother did,' said Ferry. 'She never forgave me. It seems I didn't do very much right. I abandoned everyone. I wasn't keeping a close enough eye on you when it happened. And I never understood what she saw in your father.'

Ferry had always found reasons to keep his distance, but Lev didn't want to raise that now. He couldn't see his grandfather's face; it was dark, and his body was angled away, but the sound of his voice was enough.

There was no point wanting to change the past, he said. If you could do that, he probably wouldn't be here now. Beside him, on this tiny handkerchief balcony in Vienna. On his way to Kato.

And when Ferry didn't reply, he took his hand.

By the time Lev reached Kato's pitch the next day, it was early afternoon. When she spotted him, she stood up with a smile; going away had been worth it for that alone, he thought: to see the joy on her face.

He leaned on the parapet again and watched her work. This time, he studied the emerging picture. First Kato drew a grid for the proportions, then she sketched out the image, and only then did she start applying colour. A photograph of the original lay beside her, Botticelli's Venus rising from a shell, from the sea, with her long, red hair and swan neck, head tilted to one side, firm round breasts.

Lev couldn't read the expression on the goddess's face; she looked self-absorbed but perhaps she too was filled with expectation.

Crouched beside the canvas, Kato reminded him of the girl she had been when they first met, with tatty clothes and that clever, aloof, slightly harried look. The girl who spent her afternoons on a garden swing, who used to draw at breaktime, visibly trying not to look lost – to this day, he felt ashamed of having left her on her own.

She was wearing her work clothes, as she called them. Jeans, T-shirt or jumper, sometimes overalls, so she didn't have to wash things so often. Over the years she had developed routines and an ability to organise herself and could spot a good pitch instinctively. Good meant a street with a lot of pedestrians, wide, clean pavements, and light. (Lev thought all the streets here bright and clean; he'd never seen such streets.) First you needed a permit, and then you had to get into the good books of the shopkeepers, pastors, taxi drivers, ice-cream sellers, street sweepers, everyone who had some kind of stake in a place – often not the people you might assume.

Kato concentrated on her work, looking up only when someone gave money. Lev wondered whether these moments of connection were part of her success; even after all this time, there was no guarantee that her work would be valued. People stood to watch, some for just a few seconds; others, like the older lady in the summer coat, came every day to follow the progress of a picture. A dog broke loose and sat down on the woman handing Venus a robe. Kato laughed and let it happen; the owner dropped a banknote in her basket.

When she created a picture, she said, she hoped viewers would get to the other side. It wasn't sufficient to look at it from above, making sense of the relationship between lines and colours, judging whether it was good or bad, whether you liked it or not. A picture was only right, Kato said, if you could see our world through the eyes of its subject.

Lev kept an eye on the picture when Kato went to the toilet – that used to be Tom's job. He fetched coffee, got them something to eat. And as the sun drifted across the square and boats passed by, a world of serenity and beauty opened up amid the city's bustle; if you just kept still for a while, it was revealed.

That evening they went to a lakeside park, with the trolley and the money Kato had collected that day. She didn't count it in public. When large notes dropped into the basket, she took them out at once. Over the years, she had been robbed several times.

On the way there, he'd noticed a huge cedar growing in a public square and pocketed a pine cone. In a nearby pavilion, couples were dancing to music from a cassette recorder. Two boys on skateboards passed so close that Lev had to step out of their way. At the kiosk they bought crisps and beer; this time Lev paid.

'But you're my guest,' she protested.

This far, he thought, he'd been more of an onlooker.

The colour of the lake surprised him, the clarity of the Alps that summer evening. A lake, so they say, reflects the colour of the sky, but could the sky here really be so utterly different from the sky in the Maramureş? As Kato spread a blanket on the grass by the marina, he opened her box of chalks.

Ultramarine, too dark.

Turquoise was close.

With teal mixed into it.

The lake changed colour every day, she told him, levering open the beer bottle caps with her lighter. The park was filling with people, alone or in pairs; one group had a guitar. Others swam, hired boats, walked their dogs. After his second beer, Lev needed to relieve himself, and Kato explained where the public toilet was. She told him not to be surprised by the blue light, it was to stop junkies finding a vein. When he came back, she had stretched out on the blanket and lit a roll-up with a strange smell.

A challenging smile played about her lips. She inhaled, held the smoke in her lungs and blew it slowly out. The filter, a rolled-up piece of card, was pointing at him as she passed him the cigarette. She watched him take a drag, told him he needed to smoke differently, inhale a lot of air, and then asked if he had any idea what he was smoking. Lev shook his head, took another drag, and then it dawned on him.

He had never smoked weed.

But it seemed like a good evening for a first time.

Kato whistled, thumb and forefinger in her mouth.

A woman turned around.

'So you're Lev,' she said, sitting down with them.

He couldn't work out the subtext: I've heard a lot about you? You look different to how I imagined? Anything was possible. Warja – her name was all he learned at first, because then she and Kato chatted, one question prompting another, one topic leading to the next – had to be in her mid to late thirties like them, spoke German with a hint of dialect, and touched Kato's arm absent-mindedly as she talked; little reassuring, familiar gestures that perhaps concealed some uncertainty.

'I've been to Romania,' said Warja, turning to him. 'To Bucharest, for a conference.'

Lev asked what she thought, and she said she'd liked the city's architecture, the way you could see history, decay and modernity all at once. She had been struck by the Romanians' subtle sense of irony, their humour and hospitality. She liked that mannered, discreet quality they had, but sometimes she'd found it hard to deal with, sometimes you just wanted them to get to the point. People barely acknowledged each other in public spaces, and even café waiters treated their customers with studied indifference. It was virtually impossible to catch anyone's eye.

Not impossible, but impolite, said Lev.

Warja laughed. He could imagine how different the place had seemed to her. The conversations he'd had on the train had already given him the notion that all travellers represent their country to some degree. But could individual people and experiences stand for the whole? Wallachia was different from the Banat or Bukovina, Transylvania was different from the Maramureş – so he said little, partly also because his mouth was horribly dry.

Warja had brought grapes and washed them in one of the fountains you found everywhere in this city.

Lev and Kato took some and said thank you almost in unison.

Always thanking people for food: that was Southeastern Europe, too.

A blackbird landed on the mast of a boat on the twilit lake. Its fitful movements gave it a surprised, astonished look. Its beak was a vivid orange, and so were the rings around its pupils. It balanced on the mast; each time it turned to look in a different direction, it leapt into the air like an acrobat.

They were sitting facing the lake now, Kato in the middle. Was she too thinking about Camil? Every blackbird sang of him, his love for these birds, his disappearance. After Camil, Kato had stopped painting. She started destroying the pictures from her time with him, so whenever Lev went to her house, he smuggled a few out. He hadn't cared about her art before, but with Camil gone, he felt responsible. He rescued bird pictures, early landscape sketches and her first experiments with paint, which had seemed perfect even then – but no matter what he said, or how much he encouraged her, she wouldn't go near her paints.

He recalled the postcard from Budapest, a café scene, blurred but so lifelike he thought he could see her excitement in every line. It was spring, Tom and Kato had been travelling for six months, their savings gone and, as she admitted, some days they ate only pasta or rice. Kato started drawing again; on Heroes' Square, on the Fisherman's Bastion, and passers-by threw money like a tribute.

Sing, thought Lev, sing – and as if the blackbird on the mast could hear his thoughts (this idea suddenly plausible), it burst into song. It strung its melody between boats and buildings, measuring out the space, and at once all other sounds diminished, as if someone was dialling them down to focus attention on the bird. Everything that was not part of its song slipped away. And everything that remained was part of its song.

Lev listened and looked at the fountains and the bobbing boats, at Kato and Warja, who were acting like old friends; he felt a lightness, a taking-flight sensation in his stomach, a tingling in fingertips and legs. Each moment, he thought, contained everything that had ever been, and yet held a new beginning, over and over again.

The next day, Kato took him to her Land Rover.

Approaching the car, her pace quickened. Unlocking the rear door on the passenger side, she announced: 'My home!' She reeled off the technical data, leaving him in no doubt about its advantages: off-road vehicle, all-wheel drive, six-cylinder petrol engine, and okay, it was getting on a bit, but drove like a dream, and even in third gear it could take corners at 30km/hr. The only downside: fuel consumption was insanely high.

Lev nodded appreciatively. The cream-coloured Land Rover had bars over its headlights and a spare tyre mounted on the bonnet. A retrofitted luggage rack stretched the whole length of the roof. You had to duck to get inside, and it took a while for the hot air to disperse when you opened the doors, but it had everything: bed, kerosene stove, pans and crockery, storage crates that doubled as a table or stool, scattered with papers and drawings.

These were very different from the pictures she painted on the street: landscapes, plants, still lives, portraits. You could see the direction and length of the lines, the force, the spontaneity. They were both newly drawn and also still being drawn, because the eye could not stop completing what was incomplete. He knew what art meant to her. That silent obsession that had sometimes unsettled him had been within her from the start. Looking at these pictures, it felt as though the things themselves, the woman on the bus, the cicada's wing, grasses, spider's webs – they wanted to be noticed, captured, rescued and carried over into another life and another time.

While Kato made tea, he sat on the mattress and contemplated the library on the edge of the bed: Harper Lee, Lucian Blaga, poetry by R.S. Thomas, Nelly Sachs, Nora Iuga, Adam Zagajewski, art by Jan Vermeer, Andy Warhol, Berthe Morisot.

She was studying Vermeer right now, Kato told him. How did he manage to bring action to life using mere hints? Other painters of his time worked with fine brushstrokes, but Vermeer avoided lines. 'Look here,' she said, turning to a particular page, 'he extends the skin's thin, glowing glaze out into the dark background, so the woman's face looks slightly blurred, translucent.'

Back in the day, there were no books in your house.'

'Let's not start any sentences with "back in the day".'

Her words stung, but he agreed.

Back in those days they'd known nearly everything about each other, and the Now had to cope with the comparison. That was hard enough.

'How much leave do you have?' Kato inquired.

'As much as I want.'

She stirred sugar into her tea and kept stirring long after it had dissolved.

Lev remembered asking Imre if he could take a few weeks off to visit Kato. His boss and friend hesitated a second before replying, and Lev worried that he hadn't picked a good time, but all Imre said was, 'I thought you'd never ask.'

Photos and postcards were tucked into the car widows: Kato and Tom with bikes on a mountain pass, Kato at a party in a floor-length dress, Kato and Lev on their train trip to the Black Sea. He could scarcely believe she'd kept that one all these years. He and Kato were looking expectantly into the camera; a woman from Dresden sitting in their compartment had taken the snap. How young they looked. How isolated. He was embarrassed by his haircut, his high hopes, his lack of courage. That trip had been a first departure. At the time, he had long known that Kato wanted to go away, but he'd shrugged off her hints, convinced himself she wouldn't leave.

He found more photos, realising that she couldn't talk about her memories any other way, that the world she'd left had not changed, must not change, because she too sought reassurance in what had been.

Lev reached into his trouser pocket and handed her the key.

Disbelief, consternation crossed her face.

'I don't want it,' said Kato, but took it all the same.

Whatever she said, he wasn't going to take it back.

He had carried it long enough.

Kato sliced bread and cheese. Opened the jar of zacusa that his mother had given him for her, filled little bowls with olives and figs. The key found its way onto the tray like a piece of cutlery. The roof with its luggage rack was a mobile terrace, four metres square. The city added a distant polyphony to the scene, its base whisper of bustle. The sky, still glowing blue, ended at the horizon in a line of orange.

It was time to ask about Tom.

'He stayed in Freiburg,' she said, her tone surprisingly matter-of-fact. 'We were there for nearly a year and were going to move on to France (Paris, finally!), but he'd had enough of being on the road. He wants to open a bike shop.'

She hadn't thought too hard about his announcement at first, she said. In hindsight, she was astonished at how long she had managed to put off the inevitable. As if you could stop something long since decided. It had not been an easy separation, Tom had let her keep the dream machine, and she had finally moved on, into Switzerland, then here for the last three months.

Lev looked at the city lights with her, the only patch of black being the lake. Like a hole, he thought, swallowing everything.

Kato picked up the key, turning it in her hand as if its purpose eluded her. She told him that in Freiburg, she had started teaching. A cultural association approached her in the street, and she said yes right away. First a school holiday course, then weekly street art classes for young people.

'I think that's what I want to do: teach.'

He almost choked on an olive. He had always known it –

ever since their class teacher sent her to give him lessons at his sick bed. He wasn't going to say a thing, but his smile probably gave him away; he was grinning all over his face. He wanted to know more, but Kato changed the subject, asking if there was a woman in his life. It was an off-hand question, but he knew her well enough to know it had been on her mind since they had met up.

'Not any more,' he said.

'So how… What's her name?'

'Marinela.'

Speaking her name, those familiar four syllables, brought her back in all her sensuality, honesty and seriousness. It had taken him a long time to get over her. If you really ever could get over someone.

'How did you meet?'

'On a cycling tour,' said Lev, and ignored her surprise. Some things he didn't want to share. Not yet.

In the middle of the night someone knocked on the window.

'Anyone in there?'

Kato motioned Lev to be quiet.

A torch lit up the inside of the car, but the curtains were closed, and its beam didn't reach the bed. After a while the man gave up, an engine started, headlights swept the windscreen, then it was silent again.

That was the second time a police patrol had come round, said Kato; she wasn't permitted to camp here. She would have to find another place to park, which was a shame, because of the view if nothing else.

After this incident, he found it hard to get back to sleep. He didn't dare move. When she said he could sleep there, he'd hesitated; the mattress was one metre twenty wide at most and it would be almost impossible to avoid constantly touching. The light cotton duvet wasn't really enough for two. And Kato was generous with everything but bedcovers, he knew that already.

'It wasn't just the bike shop. Tom fell in love.'

He didn't say that he had guessed as much.

The darkness diminished, gradually revealing their outlines.

'Our time was over, plus…' she hesitated.

'Yes?'

She thought about it, and after a while said: 'If I hadn't met him, I might never have had the courage to paint again. There's so much I wouldn't have learned. Every country, every city, every picture was showing me who I am. What's important to me.'

They were so close that her hair touched his cheek. He stroked her forehead tentatively, relieved to be talking as they used to back in the day – up they came, those forbidden words.

'And did you find that out?' Lev asked.

She nodded.

'I had to go away to find out.'

'I know that now.'

The morning began with an announcement.

'I'm starting a new picture today.'

Lev, who was watching her pack her things, asked about the canvas.

'There isn't one, I'll use the street.'

She created her pictures with chalk pastels containing neither wax nor oil, just compressed pigment. 'This one here,' she said, holding out a stick of chalk on the bus from the Käferberg into the city centre, 'could be the Sacré-Coeur, and this one, this blue, looks like the water of the Iza on a summer's day.'

The couple in the two seats facing theirs eyed them with interest. After the police patrol in the night, they had switched from German to Romanian. Their language opened up different spaces; one word touched another, alive, familiar. The words were worn from use, they had corners, a life of their own. But they felt right. As if until this moment, they had been viewing their memories from the outside.

On Kato's pitch by the Fraumünster a mime artist was frozen mid-movement, you couldn't see him breathe or blink. He was entirely golden: face, hands, shirt, trousers, shoes, even the chair he was sitting on, the book he was reading. When Kato informed him that this was her spot, he didn't react.

This guy has drawn a bad hand, thought Lev, he just doesn't know it yet. He sat down on a bench a little way off, curious how things would turn out. Eventually the mime released himself from his frozen state. To Lev's surprise he smiled and said something that made Kato laugh, too.

The man gathered up his equipment.

Lev offered him something to eat, but he shook his head.

It would ruin his makeup.

Kato made a rough sketch, without standing up once for

an overview of the picture. She knelt on the floor, leaning on one hand, shifting fluidly from one leg to the other, concentrating. No one stopped. Outside the nearby register office, newlyweds were being greeted with sparkling wine and flowers. A boat full of tourists passed, heading for the lake. The sun hit Lev's bench; cracks appeared in the golden man's face, as if the skin itself was breaking open. The mime artist got up and placed himself beside Kato, like someone admiring the picture.

Lev stood too, which neither of the others seemed to notice, and on impulse crossed the square to enter the church. Walking down the rows of pews, he discovered the stained-glass windows in the quire, where the ceiling was painted with stars. From outside the windows were grey and nondescript, giving no hint of what awaited you there. Visitors lit candles and talked in whispers; Lev barely noticed them. He sat and contemplated the windows until he thought he'd discovered all the characters and stories in them.

Art was a game of showing and concealing. Life, too? There was the visible and the invisible, and so little ever came to light. Some things you could hide within yourself, until you forgot they were ever there. Others you couldn't.

'How much longer are you going to wait?' his mother had asked when more post arrived from Kato.

He had been angry for a moment, but the urgency in her voice made him brush that aside. He tried to explain that he couldn't leave just like that, but she interrupted. She'd had enough of his excuses, the sawmill wouldn't go bankrupt, everything would carry on without him. His mother said he should go, Imre said he should go, everything was nudging him, urging him to leave.

Why hadn't he set out earlier?

What had he been afraid of?

City noise surged beyond the windows, but inside the church was cool and silent. Images surfaced: a bed on wheels, a tunnel filling with water, a grey sheepskin waistcoat, Lonja with a bag of nuts. He had never succeeded in putting these early losses behind him. Everything was an echo of these experiences, leading back, linking to them. He could never change them; they remained locked up inside him (or was he locked up inside them?) and there was nothing he could do about it. When memories beset him, he always pushed them away, though it felt as if he was hacking off tree branches that immediately grew back. His legs turned numb, a familiar sensation, a pull coming from deep underground, but this time he didn't fight it. He surrendered to the images, to the fear and the sadness, made no effort to stand, just let them come. Everything could move around you, pass you by, or you could become movement yourself until everything else stood still.

Someone touched his shoulder, but turning he saw only a man whose rucksack might have brushed him. Underneath the ladder to heaven, Jacob was fighting the angel. And although they were wrestling, it looked like an embrace.

Stepping back out into the square, it took Lev a while to get used to the brightness. A portrait of a young woman had taken shape on the pavement between church and river. She was wearing a turban, the blue summer shade of the Iza, overlaid with a shining yellow cloth. The woman was turning to look at the viewer, her lips slightly parted. Was she about to say something, or had she just made a remark that still echoed in the room?

Kato deepened light and shade as the golden man watched motionless over her shoulder. Passers-by paused, formed a semi-circle, threw money into the basket. As time passed, something shifted, and Lev began to see everything – Kato, the mime, the pedestrians, the square and the church – through the eyes of the woman whose pearl earring gleamed against her neck.

Finally Kato stood up and retreated a few paces. She looked happy and exhausted. The man in gold dared to move. There was a spontaneous round of applause; the two took a bow. Lev joined in, like someone out for a Saturday afternoon stroll on the river promenade, like someone who knew nothing about this woman. He was proud of Kato. Of what she had achieved, and of what lay ahead, and he could feel that her talent would carry her all her life.

Kato shared the takings with the mime.

'That's very generous,' he said, surprised.

Lev caught Kato's eye and smiled, knowing what she was going to say.

'I was born on a Saturday,' said Kato.

The man, of course, didn't have a clue what she meant.

Something was holding Lev back. A hand clutching his shoulder, though there was no one in sight. Smell of woodsmoke, hoofbeats. He gripped the ladder, set one foot on it. That weight again.

He took off his clothes, feeling lighter with every item he threw off. Now he could do it. Climbing quickly, on and on, through sunlight, through night, until the brightness returned and he reached the top. Then he pulled up the ladder and leaned it against a tree. He was in a forest, but no leaves, birds or wind were to be heard, just a distant murmur. Rocks rose out of a lake and women sat on them combing their hair, which drifted down into the valleys as mist. They were dressed in cloudy white, with little bells on their ankles. One of them turned to him, pointing her hand, and he took it as a direction. A light was burning on the far side of the lake. He started walking.

In the morning, he woke late. He could hear from the passing cars that the roads were wet. The mist from his dream had floated into the city, a light, damp mist that muffled all sounds. After breakfast he began to pack. Each action led to the next, made it necessary. He handed the room key in at reception, stepped out onto the street.

The Land Rover was parked outside the guesthouse. No doubt about it: he knew no other car with barred headlights.

He knocked on the passenger window.

Kato leaned over the seat, wound the window down. 'What's up? Aren't you getting in?'

He got in. Threw the holdall behind him.

Kato greeted him with a kiss.

How had she known he'd made a decision? Why was she in such an exuberant mood?

'Ready to go?' she asked.

He nodded.

'Good,' she said, and started the car.

When they had left the city behind, Lev asked:

'Where are we going?'

Kato turned up the music.

'You choose.'

Pictures of You

Seven

Kato pulled the door shut carelessly, as if she'd be back in a few hours. She didn't even turn the key.

A door closing should make different sounds, thought Lev, depending on whether it was to be opened again a short while later, or closed indefinitely. Why couldn't he hear the difference? The door creaked as usual as it dragged across the top wooden step, before a little groan, almost a cough, signalled that it was closed.

He wanted to ask if she was coming back.

But the door wasn't saying.

It refused its complicity.

Kato looked changed: the village, the house, perhaps even Lev, had already vanished from her face, the way she moved. Her eyes flickered with the brightness of departure and beginning.

'Thank you for coming,' she said.

How formal it sounded.

For a moment, Lev allowed himself to believe this wasn't a parting. In a few days, the door would be open again, this openness would be tangible, would call to him, and Kato would be back at the table, in the room containing nothing superfluous, nothing that wasn't useful. They had tried to make these two rooms more homely, painted the walls, washed rugs down by the mill, bought new crockery and got rid of everything that had belonged to her father, his clothes and tools. Lev had wanted to banish the darkness that had always reigned here.

Now the table was cleared, the door closed. Now a man was sitting on the trunk of the pear tree a storm had uprooted the previous autumn, never looking away as Kato stowed something in her bike pannier. Did Tom fear she would change her mind?

Lev couldn't even say that he didn't like him. Had they met under different circumstances, he would have admired Tom for being so well-travelled and independent. Perhaps. But now, all he could think was: Why did you have to come through here, of all places? Why our village?

'I think I've got everything,' said Kato.

'If we need anything, we'll buy it.'

'What might we need?'

'Precisely.'

Tom laughed.

Kato handed Lev the house key.

As always, he was the first to look away, to release a hug, to break the silence.

'Send me postcards from each country.'

All at once, he couldn't wait to get it over with.

'I promise,' she said.

He could still hear the soft echo of the words.

Lev left Kato's plot of land, which lay down a side street on the outskirts of the village, and headed up the hill. When he turned round, all he could see was the dust trail from their bike wheels. You should have looked, he thought, if only to see whether she glanced back at you. Everything lay hazy and washed out before him: scattered smallholdings with steep shingled roofs, streets, paths, wooded hills, mountains, everything fitted into the familiar picture yet at the same time seemed to be drifting apart, as if someone was pulling at the ends – like his mother pulling the wool back out of an errant stitch.

Every hill, every mountain afforded a view of the next, forming a long chain of reassurance. Something else would come, he wasn't walking into nothingness, even if that was exactly what he feared now. He ignored the path, breathing through his open mouth, and with each ascent, each descent, something was lost, something in him grew weaker, smaller. He had shrunk to an insignificant dot, no different from that rock, or the motionless lizard sunning itself there. He longed to do likewise, to feel the rock's warmth, become a rock, part of the landscape, surrendering to summers and winters, the cycles of light and night.

Flopping onto the grass, he felt solid ground, ants on his skin. The wind picked up, no longer a soft breeze but racing, falling. It pushed against his body, his eyelids. Lev pressed his hands into the grass.

The ant walks across your arm and doesn't know it; the wind falls on the hills without knowing it; but you, you know. She is gone.

Tom had come riding his bike through the village the week before. People came out of their houses to admire this apparition. Long hair, tanned skin, muscular yet slight. His T-shirts were made of thin fabric in garish colours, and his legs wore what looked like cut-off tights. Functional wear, said Anuța – of all people – authoritatively. Aside from 'thank you' and 'hello', Tom didn't speak a word of Romanian; he got by with German and English, and when neither worked, used his smile, his hands. He had a smile that was answer enough.

People invited him in, as they would any traveller; they had him tell stories, wanting to know everything. Tom seemed used to being the centre of attention, accepted every invitation, ate, drank, told stories, smiled, stayed in guest beds, hay barns, or in his tent. Kato was there from the day he arrived, translating, never leaving his side.

Tom set no store by conventions; he was charmingly ill-mannered and ignored rules that everyone in the valley abided by. Yet beside him they looked like country bumpkins, backward, almost grey, as if with his garish T-shirts Tom had taken all the colour for himself.

The children liked him, touching his skin and stroking his hair as if he was a saint from the church come to earth. They sat on his lap, wanted to ride on the pannier rack. They said he was a good storyteller even when they didn't understand a word; they said he had been halfway round the world. Eighty worlds around the day – or something like that.

Tom came from Hamburg and had been cycling across Europe for a year, a different, greater Europe stretching from the Atlantic to the Black Sea. He had cycled through the states that once made up East Germany, then Poland, Ukraine and the Republic of Moldova, and was heading back west through northern Romania (where the nail holds up the map, as the locals said).

In Warsaw he had worked in a greenhouse cutting flowers, until he got an itchy rash. He'd been a caretaker in the reopened Saharna monastery, and on Lake Yalpuh spent two months working for a fisherman. He stayed as long as he liked, travelled wherever he liked, sold his story to local papers. Tom seemed to have no obligations, no concern about money. He had one of those faces you couldn't imagine getting worry lines.

Kato's interest in Tom had not escaped Lev. Her eyes acquired a haunted, feverish look; perhaps she had known it at once. Tom was her escape, her means of getting away. Lev had brushed off Kato's unrest, her growing dissatisfaction. He didn't want to see that she was unhappy, just as, even today, he hadn't wanted to see that she was going away.

'Why don't we leave,' she had suggested. 'Head off somewhere without knowing when we'll come back.'

'We can't,' said Lev.

'We can't, or you don't want to?'

Tom took a liking to the young woman who followed him everywhere. Kato declared without further ado that she wanted to go with him. And all Tom said was: You'll be needing a bike, then. Kato got hold of a bike, one that actually looked rideable, Tom inspected it, bought panniers, and Lev was glad that no one asked him to help. He had always helped Kato, but this time he didn't offer.

They practised on the bikes.

Slalom lines, dirt roads.

Ringing laughter.

'Do you want to sleep with me?' Tom had apparently asked, so polite in this matter where usually urgent hands sufficed, or looks that made you feel you were already naked.

'And?' Lev had said.

'And what?'

'Did you sleep with him?'

He must have used the wrong tone, because she didn't reply.

Lev wasn't going to make it easy for her. When she informed him that she was going away with Tom, he looked at her coldly. He was overcome with the need to drive her even further away, to put an unbridgeable distance between them. He wanted that disappointment in her face to stick. The worst thing would be for her feelings about him to vanish at the first bend in the road. He took his time, laboriously beating the dust from his trousers and wishing her a safe journey, with a look that deliberately missed her eyes.

The next day, he couldn't force himself out of bed.

Was he sick, his mother asked.

He gave her to understand that he wanted to be alone.

As a child, he'd been confined to bed after an accident; at the time it had felt like a punishment, but now this was what he wanted. Not to have to get up, to lie and listen to the house shifting from day to night, his mother's footsteps in the main room, on the loggia, in the summer kitchen, until evening when everything grew quieter and finally there was no movement of any kind in the house or courtyard. His sister Bredica would visit, his niece and nephews, his brothers. 'Get up!' they would say, and he would ask, what for?

When Lis sat on his bed that evening, he found the courage to look at her. She kissed his forehead; he was embarrassed and yet not embarrassed. Who was allowed to do that, if not her.

'I know you're staying on my account.'

Lev sat upright. Was that what she thought?

'But she has no one left here.'

'What about me?' said Lev.

'You can't both stay for each other's sake.'

Backstreet noises, yard gates, dogs barking, a bucket striking the rim of a well. Coming to examine his room, the evening sun laid a veneer of levity over the furniture.

'Come and eat,' said Lis. 'Tomorrow, when Kato sets off, go and wish her well and give her this from me.'

Lev took the envelope she handed him.

His mother was already at the door when he said she was wrong about one thing. He wasn't staying on her account; he had other reasons.

He didn't say what they were.

He didn't talk about Kato. When others chatted about where she and Tom might be, he feigned indifference and changed the subject. He went out to work and brought sawdust back on his shoes and clothes; he completed countless tasks, forgotten even as he was doing them. Resistance attached itself to every movement, every decision, like an additional weight. All at once it was an effort to get dressed, to hold a cup, to leave the house. If something fell on the floor, it was almost impossible to pick it up. It had wanted to fall. Why make the effort?

He had wished her well, at least.

One thing he didn't have to reproach himself for.

On the day when Lev just stood watching a gang saw jammed in a trunk, Imre sent him home. Moving at immense speed, the blades overheated and warped; trunks started backing up on the conveyor belt. All it would take to stop the machine was an outstretched hand, but he couldn't make himself do it. In fact, he would have liked to wait until the whole thing sprang apart. The machine was rebelling, it was on his side, unlike Kato's front door.

Imre didn't ask what was wrong. He looked at him, as if Lev's posture, his eyes, the way he was standing by the machine, told him everything he needed to know.

'Don't come back until you've got over it.'

On the way home, Lev made a decision: what if he got himself a bike, too? He would take some leave, and go south, not west.

Not towards her, but away from her.

Not out of this country.

Into it.

Were bikes suddenly in fashion now, Sigi asked. People were like birds in autumn, they couldn't just stay where they were, always had to be roaming around.

Everything Sigi sold came with life advice, wanted or not.

In times like these, it was extremely difficult to be constantly (he stressed the word) getting hold of bikes.

'Can you find me one, or not?'

Sigi looked offended, though in fact he always looked like that, as if someone had just done him a disservice. Perhaps it was because he'd lost all his teeth, and, since losing all his teeth, could take no real pleasure in food.

'Alright then,' said Lev, making as if to leave. That was the best way to speed up the transaction, though it couldn't be deployed too soon or you would take all the fun out of it for Sigi.

'Difficult, I said, not impossible!'

Lev collected his bike a few days later, paying a sum that seemed unreasonable for a rusty old bizikel, and the next morning he set off. His mother had responded to news of his trip only by raising her eyebrows, but that evening he found a rucksack, towel and soap on his bed. He set off early, to avoid a never-ending series of farewells, locked the door of Kato's house, and put the key in his trouser pocket. For a moment he was tempted to go in, but just straightened the faded picture of the Eiffel Tower in the window from the outside.

Would her trip take her as far as Paris?

On Kato's thirtieth birthday they had travelled to the Black Sea together. The train was packed and rarely exceeded fifty kilometres an hour; all the signs and information were in German. Every village, no matter how small, had a station and signalman. Every person who got off gave their ticket to someone getting on.

When a football team of small boys embarked just before Sibiu and the other passengers let them sit on their laps, Lev and Kato gave up their seats and sat on the floor. You could open the door while the train was moving. Kato closed her eyes in the wind; light and dark shadows passed over her face. Somewhere between Braşov and Sinaia, the guard played a song by The Cure over the loudspeakers. They talked to a passenger from Dresden about the war in the Balkans, which had once again been about aligning supposed ethnic borders with national borders. They came to the conclusion that their nationality was less important than the network of disparate influences that was evolving all the time, woven from music, stories, sayings.

Whenever he heard The Cure, Lev remembered that train journey. And if he had to pick a moment when he thought everything was possible for them, it was then.

He spent the first night in a hay loft.

He had ham, bread and eggs from home, and bought milk and cheese from a woman. When she offered to put him up for the night, he said he had to keep going. He couldn't say where to. She looked at him as if he was not in his right mind. People round here didn't just go for a ride. What must she have thought of him in that sweat-drenched shirt, the bike with its split saddle, his few possessions in a rucksack? The first stage had been the hardest. Hair pin bends wound uphill, and when he reached the top, stiff-legged, and looked out over the rolling land ahead, he doubted he would last long. His backside wouldn't, at any rate. But then came a downhill section, and in the end he rode further than he'd imagined.

He didn't want company, but when he thought of the woman now, her friendly but serious eyes, her upright, approachable posture, he wasn't sure he had made the right decision.

Before him lay a valley with a scattering of farmsteads and black water buffalo, keeping a measured distance from one another. He had left the Wooded Carpathians behind on the first day. But not Kato. He had learned to see the landscape as it appeared in her drawings, long lines, denser places, colours running together. When he felt the rush of air on his skin as he rode, dust burning in his eyes, he was close to her. She too had rushing air and dust in her face; she too had to get used to the monotony of the movement, legs always moving the same way, leaning forward, arms outstretched.

How far had they gone that first week? Did she have everything she needed? Could she keep up with Tom? What was going through her mind? Was she thinking: turn around, keep going? He had no idea.

Looking after her had become a habit. He bought her groceries, fixed dripping taps, replaced floorboards; he helped her deal with officials, no matter how often she told him she would be fine on her own. Now he could no longer help. He didn't even know where she was. In leaving, she had taken something with her, a meaning, a joy, and he couldn't talk about it, because nobody else could feel it.

Before it got completely dark, he made a pile of hay and lay down to sleep. The only sound was the wood creaking in the wind and warmth. The rucksack of provisions hung on a hook. The mice would have to find something else to eat.

The next morning, he pulled the door of the hay loft closed and rode on without any breakfast. His legs were stiff, reluctant to fall into the rhythm. The first hill was also a little too steep for this particular morning. On the spur of the moment, he turned around.

She was sitting on the covered bench by her gate, cleaning corncobs and watching him approach. She showed no surprise as she stood up. Curtains twitched in the house next door. In the middle of the courtyard stood a cow with a colourless coat and stunted front legs. The sight was only disconcerting for a second; since Chernobyl, they had all got used to deformed animals. A chained dog leapt up and sprang towards Lev barking, but stopped at a sign from the woman. She went into the house, brought soap and a towel. He didn't say that he had both.

He washed his face at the well, noticing that the pump was stiff, used the long-drop toilet and combed his hair in front of a mirror nailed to a plank wall. She laid the table on the veranda and fixed her eyes on him as he walked the full length of the yard to meet her. Lev pretended not to notice her looking as he climbed the veranda steps; he found it both unnerving and flattering.

Her name was Marinela and she was around forty. Her eyebrows were barely there, her lips almost the same tone as her skin. He could only guess at the colour of the hair under her headscarf. Did she manage the land and the animals by herself? He hadn't seen anyone else, yesterday or today. A bead curtain obscured the view into the house.

He asked if she lived alone here, and she said her husband worked in Italy and the children had moved to Iaşi. She paused at the end of each sentence, as if momentarily unable to connect it to the next. Her voice was clear, but with a depth in which the words echoed.

Wasn't she lonely here, Lev asked, and regretted it at once. But she answered bluntly, without hesitation. 'No lonelier than before.'

Lev ate bread, tomatoes, unsalted sheep's cheese, and drank coffee that she brought out from the kitchen in a pan, the bead curtain fizzing each time she passed. She just drank coffee, holding the cup and never setting it down.

Riding around must be lonely, too, she said with a smile, as if she had caught him out. Some people 'care umblă cu cioara vopsită' – went about with a painted crow. They were feigning something. But he had no painted crow, she said; the one riding with him was black.

The next few days took him past meadows, fields of maize and hemp. He kept finding himself in flocks of sheep, woolly backs flowing and parting like water around an obstacle in a stream. The land grew flatter, the fruit trees more numerous. He had arrived in Transylvania. Siebenbürgen.

'Erdély', said Imre in Hungarian.

'Ardeal', said his siblings in Romanian.

Lev knew the area from his trips to Sighişoara. But cycling was different. He saw derelict apartment blocks, factory buildings that had clearly been abandoned, rusting cranes and disused conveyor belts, towering chimneys. The architecture of recent decades expressed boundless desolation; these buildings would keep the past on view for years to come. But there were also signs of new beginnings. Houses with only one storey finished were sometimes already inhabited, second-floor walls rising up with no roof. Small shops had plastic chairs beneath parasols printed with beer adverts. In villages built along a single street, people sat outside their houses as they always had done, lives facing outwards. But there were fewer of them now.

Lev remembered a conversation with his brother Valea, who never failed to remind him that they were half brothers. You Germans live on a street, surgically attached to your houses, you close your curtains and hide in your yards like a fox in his hole. But us Romanians live *in* the street, for everyone to see and speak to. If the street should tilt and slide away, we slide with it. If your street, your house, were taken away, what would you be then? – Even now, the way his brother distinguished 'us' from 'you' stung.

The water was low in the rivers, and plastic rubbish snagged in trees and bushes. The lanes crackled when the wind blew. Lev stayed off the main roads, followed fences; sometimes a track ended in rough ground, and he had to get off and push. He helped himself to apples and plums when he was hungry, and he was always hungry. No real thoughts, beyond eating and sleeping. No plans, beyond managing the next ascent, quenching his thirst. His legs had grown used to the new movement and only his arms were stiff. He tried riding hands-free, which was not an immediate success.

There was always a well to drink from, always someone who would feed him and let him stay overnight in the barn. Once, Lev slept under a yew tree. The needles, dark green with a lighter underside, shimmered or rustled (he tried to find the right word). He couldn't block out sounds; they went right through him, just fleeting and forceful enough to translate into words and images.

Once, he'd tried to explain to Kato how it felt.

Had it always been like that, she'd asked.

Sometimes, he said, he was freed from having to listen.

When? she asked, keeping her eyes on him. Kato's eyes were as clear as the water of the Iza. He thought he should be able to see all the way to the bottom, but he never could, and so there was always a slight recoil as well.

When I'm with you.

But he hadn't said it.

The night under the yew put him in his place, tipping him back into loneliness and doubt.

What was he doing? Why was he on this ride? But every time he felt like turning around, something stopped him. Kato couldn't even tell him if she would ever return, so how could he turn back after just a few days?

Cycling through a village somewhere between Reghin and Târgu Mureş, he stopped, tired and hungry, outside the pastor's house. Dark window panes, pale yellow crumbling render. The gate was unlocked. He stepped carefully into the courtyard, knowing at once it was unoccupied. The inner courtyard was cobbled, with weeds and grass sprung up between the stones. Lady's mantle and black-eyed Susans had established themselves there. In the centre of the yard stood a nut tree; beneath it two wooden chairs, turned towards each other as if chatting. The sky was cloudless, only the haze hinted at September's arrival. The windows of the house were intact, but the elder bush would soon be taller than the roof. The building next door, probably the parish hall, was in the worst shape, with roof shingles gone and rafters exposed; a hole gaped where the door must once have been.

Everything happened by itself, the shingles falling, the growth and overgrowth. This yard was so silent, so entirely abandoned that he felt like an intruder. Then he heard a goat bleating. She looked down at him from the walls of the parish hall.

Sighişoara was the first town he didn't skirt around. He felt foreign among so many people with clean faces and fresh clothes. Scenic black and white photos of the town were on sale at the clock tower; calendars of naked women hung in the kiosk. Wooden stalls had been set up in the marketplace, and several men were warily scoping out the area. One asked him for a cigarette. Lev ate lángos and filled his water bottle from the fountain. Bells rang and, as always, reminded him of the revolution.

He strolled, seemingly without purpose, along the familiar narrow streets until he reached the apartment building. When someone walked through the door, he slipped in behind. He waited in the passage until the footsteps faded away, then went through to the rear courtyard. Several more buildings, each built up against the last, flower pots, washing lines stretched across. Steep wooden stairs led up to the first floor. A glance through the window revealed that Ferry's former workshop was now a storage room. The beech workbench was still there, where his grandfather had produced watch glasses, where they had also eaten and held parties when there wasn't enough room in the flat. Ferry had lived here with his wife, who left him when Lis was three years old. His mother had grown up here – until that harvest when she fell in love with Lev's father and moved two hundred kilometres north to the village.

Had his mother found it hard to leave? To exchange her familiar life for another, German for Romanian, to bring up four children, of whom only Lev was her flesh and blood? He had never considered how painful her departure must have been for Ferry.

Had he ever been back here, after he fled?

Lev picked up a piece of glass from the floor outside the workshop.

Then he heard a window opening.

What was he doing here, a man asked.

Suddenly, he was unable to keep lying to himself. He was here for a specific reason. In a restaurant toilet he washed his face, smoothed back his dusty hair. He looked at himself in the mirror, moistened his cracked lips.

Would he be eating, the waiter asked.

Maybe later, he said, and walked quickly out.

When he reached her house, he stared up at the first-floor window at which he'd so often thrown pebbles. There were still cacti on the windowsill, and behind the iron front door he heard voices, someone practising the violin. His courage left him, he turned around and walked to the Scholars' Stairway that led up to the School on the Hill. Below the wooden roof it was dusky-warm. As always, he counted the steps up to the Lyceum.

At the top he heard a familiar voice.

'It really is you.'

Astrid stood before him.

She was clutching her cardigan across her chest with one hand, though it wasn't cold.

'I saw you outside our house.'

'Yes, I…'

'Did you come to admire the view?'

Behind the trees lay the town with its narrow streets, walls and towers, its confusion of cables and television antennas. How often, visiting his grandfather, Lev had been sent to a shop for milk or bread; he spent hours queuing with other men and women who were also hoping that the sign saying 'lapte' or 'pîine' was true that day, and not a substitute – sometimes the word was all they got. People talked softly as they stood, pressed shoulder to shoulder, and when Lev thought about it now, he marvelled at this mixture of resignation, powerlessness, passivity.

'How are you, Astrid?'

'Fine,' she said, still holding her cardigan over her chest. 'I'm getting married soon.'

'I'm pleased for you,' he said, actually feeling pleased and relieved in equal measure.

'I came to ask your forgiveness.'

'That's what I hoped,' said Astrid.

At first he thought he was looking in the wrong place.

Then he had to accept that his bike was gone.

It was his punishment, it had to be a punishment, what

else. He had made his apology, but it wasn't enough, no one could get off so lightly. For a moment he was tempted to ride away on one of the other unlocked bikes. Wasn't it his due, since something of his had been taken away?

Lev left the town and walked a few kilometres before turning off the main road, crossing fields, sloping vineyards, woodland. His mind quietened and soon his head was empty, even of the question, where next? He slept on the ground, propped against the wall of an abandoned hut. In the early morning he heard footsteps, whispering. Someone prodded his arm.

Two men stood in front of him. One demanded his rucksack.

Lev got to his feet, quickly grasped who he was dealing with, lowered his head. In the military he had learned not to provoke people. There was no need to think at times like these; you knew instinctively whether talking would do any good, and whether you stood a chance in a fight. He could have tried – physically, he had the upper hand – but he saw the knife and decided against it. Aside from money, his rucksack contained nothing valuable. His identity card was in his trouser pocket. So was the key to Kato's house.

Once the men had disappeared into the fields, he stood motionless for a while. It seemed strangely fitting that everything was gone. He felt liberated, though from what he couldn't say. At least they didn't beat you up, he thought, though he'd have acquiesced in that, too.

The men's faces kept flashing before his eyes; he could picture them in detail, though he'd seen them only briefly.

Before leaving, the shorter one, who dragged one leg slightly, had nodded to him with an almost apologetic look.

What was he to do now?

His Romanian grandmother would tell him to turn back at once. She always knew what was coming. Nothing in her life had been unforeseen. Not the loss of her son, the revolution, not even her own death. Bunica saw the path of a bird through the air before it took wing.

In her final weeks she slept a lot, fitfully, feverishly. Sometimes memories surfaced; sometimes she was responsive, and her mind seemed clear. When Lev asked if death frightened her, she shook her head, as if he'd asked a particularly stupid question. She had a recurring dream, she told him. She dreamed of a candle on the windowsill. A draught blew through the room, and it went dark. But just for a moment – and then she saw the candle on the other side of the window, burning.

Only at the funeral had Lev learned her full name was Maria Aurica Costin. To him, she had always been Bunica – Grandma. Her mentioning the dead in nearly every conversation (what your father would do now; my husband always said…) had seemed like one of her quirks. Now he too had become someone who asked the dead for advice. But whatever Bunica might say, this could not be the end of his journey.

That afternoon he reached a village. At some point he couldn't tell whether he was walking into or out of it, the main street was so winding. Single-storey houses ran like a ribbon, wall to wall, gate to gate. He passed the fortress church. An older couple was sitting on a bench. Lev greeted them in

German, and without much preamble the man invited him to stay for dinner.

'You look hungry.'

'And I am.'

'He could do with a shower, as well,' his wife added.

'Yes, he could,' Lev confirmed.

The woman, who introduced herself as Anna and insisted he use her first name, laid out clean clothes for him. She would wash his things and they would be dry by lunchtime. Wherever he was going (and here she paused, giving him an opportunity to explain his strange appearance), he couldn't carry on like that. The jeans and T-shirt with a 'Levis' logo came from their son in Germany.

Anna, Herbert and one other woman were the only Transylvanian Saxons who'd stayed in the village. A few had got their houses back or bought another and now spent the summer here. 'Summer Saxons,' said Herbert, and Lev couldn't tell if he meant it disparagingly.

Lev wanted to ask why they stayed, but he didn't; instead, over dinner he told them that he had set out on a cycling holiday. Calling it a holiday felt strange; he couldn't remember ever having had a holiday, let alone needing one. He was ashamed to be making up a cover story for his journey, but he had to tell them something.

They had vegetable soup, fried sausage with mashed potato, and pickled peppers. Anna, having made soup for this workday dinner, bulked out the meal as people do when guests come. Herbert poured wine. They had two sons, a younger one whose

T-shirt Lev was wearing, and an older one with children of his own. Both lived in Stuttgart.

His bed was made up in a room overlooking the courtyard. He undressed and got into the cool, fresh sheets. When the door opened a crack and Anna asked if he needed anything else, it was all he could do to murmur 'Thank you'.

He appeared in the yard, sheepishly, at lunchtime the following day. Anna waved his embarrassment away, saying he was a good guest, he'd saved them breakfast.

As promised, his clothes were dry.

Herbert was oiling the chain of a bicycle.

'You can have it,' he said. 'None of us rides it any longer.'

He couldn't accept that, said Lev.

'Why not? It's just standing around here.'

Anna put her hands into her apron and looked at him.

Lev could only nod. His throat suddenly felt tight.

The wave of emigration was inevitable. Like an addiction.

Everyone was frightened of being the last.

Anna and Herbert had decided to stay. Their children had gone, their neighbours, even the pastor. Why were they clinging on here, people asked. They weren't clinging on, they were living, said Anna, and Lev was glad he hadn't asked that question.

A lost time, they said. As if there was a time that stayed.

Now he saw the villages he rode through on his new bike with different eyes. He'd given it little thought before; his village had its own abandoned houses, gardens run to seed. For years now, people had been giving each other the look that said:

Are you leaving, too? Outside the yard gates, on the benches, someone always had a story of someone else leaving. And with each person who left, the idea of leaving grew. And with each person who stayed, the hope of being able to stay solidified.

In a parish hall, shards of glass lay scattered on the floor like wind-blown leaves. Cracks ran across the church windows, cut ropes coiled like snakes in the bell tower. The vaulted ceiling of another church was falling down; someone had lined up plaster fragments along the pews. In the sacristy he found furniture, crates, rolled-up rugs, a wheelbarrow. The air was cool and smelled of cushions, candlewax and damp. In one village, the Orthodox congregation had moved into the Protestant church and placed icons on the altar. In another church, a man inspecting the quire had the look of a person seeking God. Lev sat in a pew, read the writing on the walls: If you do not stand firm in your faith, you will not stand at all.

Anna had packed sandwiches, cheese and peppers for him, and insisted that he keep her son's T-shirt. Perhaps, Lev speculated, she liked to think of a man cycling around in her son's shirt.

He shared his supper with a cat. Leaning, eyes closed, against the wall of a barn, he felt something warm and soft press against his legs. She was dainty and entirely black, right down to her whiskers and paws.

When someone went away, they left behind their house and friends and their animals. Lev remembered a man who couldn't bear to give his horse into a stranger's care so took it to the knacker instead. A woman who let her chickens out, knowing they wouldn't survive. He thought of Kato's love for animals. Then he remembered how Pax had been set free and laughed loud enough to frighten the black cat. He'd never asked Kato what she had done with the dog. Some things remained unspoken. And that of which you do not speak never happened.

He liked this tacit agreement of theirs, to know essential things and leave some subjects untouched. Or was he kidding himself? He had been in the forest and in the army. She had lost Camil. And what did he know of her everyday existence, of life with her father? She didn't share it, and he didn't ask – out of respect. And convenience. Over the years, the topics they didn't discuss had grown more numerous; they were planted in the ground like boundary stones, not to be passed.

Lev broke little pieces off the cheese and sausage, fed the cat. After the meal she washed herself thoroughly and lay down beside him. Her fur had a hint of purple in it, like lavender, he thought, like an aubergine. He looked out over the fields, a landscape that was managing without lights or people. They lived in an abandoned world. A world on the threshold. Kato had seen that; he hadn't.

He saw it only now, when she too had gone away.

That night in the barn he dreamed of Khalil. Of green eyes with orange-brown flecks, rimmed in black as if with his sister's kohl. When his eyes closed, all that remained was this black line rising up the sides of the nose and sweeping back across the lids. Sometimes Khalil put Lev in mind of a young dragon, and sometimes when he sat on his hind legs and puffed out his chest, he reminded him of a fine gentleman, his shirt as white as if he'd bathed in milk.

For a long time, he hadn't wanted to admit Khalil was dying; he was getting on, he told himself, the tomcat was just very old and very tired. Then Khalil grew thinner and started eating less, his appetite erratic. What he liked one day seemed to disgust him the next. One of his eyes turned red, an inflamed circle around the pupil.

Khalil lay down in the shed, where he had never lain before, behind a wooden board leaning against the wall. Lev searched for half a day before finding him there, talked to him, tried to lure him out with food, but Khalil looked at him with no expression in his red-rimmed eye, as if they didn't know each other.

Lev sat by the board and waited.

Khalil got up only to do his business. He stopped eating, his breath grew shallow and he was completely silent. Lev kept this silence, too, for two days and one night.

'All animals know how to die,' said Lis. 'It isn't something he needs your help with.'

When night fell, his brother Dorin brought a blanket out for him.

Later, the cat's breathing quickened, almost becoming a purr, though nothing like the reassuring purr he had known since childhood. He felt Khalil's struggle, a silent, hard struggle, and despaired because there was nothing he could do. He went indoors, couldn't bear it, and came back to the shed, where Khalil was lying unchanged behind the board. Eventually the cat pulled himself upright to go to the toilet and collapsed halfway. Lev carried him into the garden, shocked at how light, how almost incorporeal he was, then returned him to his spot and sat back down in front of the board. Heat and heaviness filled his chest. Tears ran down his face, though he wasn't aware he was crying. Death was in the air, filling the whole shed; no sound now but a distant crackle, like a fire burning on the other side of a door. Death was silence, was a foretaste of emptiness, taking everything away. On the last day, in Khalil's final hours, Lev tried to feed him, dripping milk into his mouth; later he reproached himself for it.

The milk trickled out of Khalil's mouth, he didn't swallow, and Lev was ashamed of the violence he was doing. He had never forced the cat to do anything, and now he was trying to force him to live.

He died while Lev was briefly in the house.

He hadn't been able to die with Lev on the other side of the board.

The colours were subdued, as if they'd faded.

Khalil was still present when he woke. Khalil meant 'good friend' in Arabic. Kato had told him a mad story all those years ago, about the cat coming from the Middle East and having an excellent pedigree. After his death Lev had been tempted to ask her about it, but really he wanted to live inside this story, even if it wasn't true.

The dark places where experience stopped and memory began were everywhere. Some things remained and some were lost, sometimes even as they happened, and however hard you tried, they would not reappear. Memories were scattered through time like clearings in the forest. You came across them by chance, never knowing what you would find there. The truly memorable moments, those that were not lost, never belonged to you alone. Only fear was yours alone. Forgetting. Everything else, thought Lev, could be retained only through others.

How had he spent these last few years?

He and Imre had privatised the sawmill; he'd looked after his niece, his nephews, visited Milena at the guesthouse. Had driven around the Iza valley with Kato, helped his mother and Bunica, spent whole days by the river – and waited. For Camil to come back, for Kato to start painting again. They had waited for the dictatorship to end, then for a new life to begin, without knowing what that would entail. They had longed for nothing more feverishly than the opening of the borders, and when it happened, they didn't know what to do. Lev no longer believed that he would be brave.

Something was holding him back.

His thoughts returned to Kato and Tom with increasing distance; he wondered merely where they might be. A few more pushes on the pedals and he knew it was time to go back. He took the direct route with long stretches on the main roads, overtaken recklessly with shouted comments veering from surprised or jocular to rude, which he countered with a victory sign. Two days later, he arrived back in the village where he had spent the first night of his journey. Marinela was not sitting by the gate. In his imagination she hadn't moved from her bench the whole time.

He knocked. The dog started barking.

When it fell silent, Lev knew she was on her way to the gate. Once again, a curtain twitched in the house next door.

That's a different bike, said Marinela in greeting, and the black crow isn't sitting on the handlebars, either.

'Yes, the crow has gone,' Lev confirmed.

'But the rider is no less cuckoo than before.'

While she cooked, he mended the stiff well pump. The cow with the colourless coat and the short forelegs watched with interest.

Marinela didn't ask why he was here; she laid the table on the veranda with the good crockery. He noticed, and saw her openly eyeing him, too. There was no calculation in Marinela's language. Hers was a language of heat and green hills, of unsparing, never-ending work, a language of the body, not the tongue.

After dinner, which they consumed in silence, broken only by half-sentences of reassurance – more salt, would you like some water, it's good, thank you – he tried to help clear up. She laid her hand on his. He felt her skin, the warm pressure of her hand, and a thought ran through him, less a thought than an image. Her expression changed, as if she too had seen this image.

Marinela showed him the shower: a rain barrel on a wooden frame with a watering-can attachment. The water was pleasantly warm; a shaving kit lay on a stool. She must have put it there while he was washing. He shaved in front of the mirror on the wooden wall and a new-looking face appeared, as it always does when a beard is removed.

The table was cleared. The dog pretended to ignore them, but went on paying attention. The cow slumped and lay down in the middle of the courtyard. Someone pulled a handcart along the village street, a rattle of cans, the smell of bonfires.

Marinela had changed her clothes, handed him a glass of schnapps. They drank standing up, and just as Lev was about to speak, to say something that would explain his being here, to justify and prolong his being here that night, she moved into the doorway, as if the crucial question had long been settled. The bead curtain flowed around her, falling in bright droplets down the length of her body. Half in the house, half on the veranda, she turned back.

Kept looking at him until he understood.

Sușia zavela vouca tai
iahnia ed vodii. Vouc sa
zoper mai edhori a iahnia
malo mai udoleni.
Vouc sa hapeu vedete ez
iahniam: 'Ta cio',
zazvidau oven 'calamuteș
vodu, cotru ia piu?'

Six

Entering was like walking into a museum. Outside might be bright daylight, it could be summer, the world might be burning, but in Bunica's parlour it was cool and dark.

The central beam split the house in half: one side for stove and bed, the other for high days and holidays. Here, a feeling of absence reigned. The furniture seemed asleep, dust motes settled, wrinkles had been smoothed from the throw on the sofa, cushions stood in obedient ranks. The room was clean and tidy, always ready for visitors, but Lev knew it preferred being alone. As children they had been convinced a ghost lived there, and when they were sent in to fetch something, they would hold their breath.

As long as they didn't breathe, nothing bad could happen.

Bunica was always in motion, from kitchen to animal stalls to barn. She had an ever-changing number of chickens, a dozen sheep that the shepherd would soon be bringing down to the pasture, and a dust-grey donkey that she called măgăruş – little donkey. Even in the late evening she didn't rest. She stood at the gate, chatting to neighbours, her white nightshirt a beacon in the twilight. She put a blanket on the table and ironed by candlelight, she took the big box radio out to the field – even if everything belonged to the Agricultural Production Cooperative, she still called it 'her field'. They had lent their fields to the state and, when it was all over, they would get them back. The radio played all night to keep wild boar away. Not Radio Free Europe, I hope, Lev had joked. The very idea, she said, the boar must remain communist, of course.

Bunica was in constant motion so the ghosts of the past could never catch up with her, nor the devil, nor fear. The dead were not dead to Bunica. To think of them as unable to slip at will between the great beyond and this world was a lack of faith, a ridiculous error. This was why she laid an extra place for every meal.

It was said that those who returned could not speak well, or at all. So how could they ask for food? Lev wondered. And did all the dead have to eat from the one plate? Bunica's husband, her son (Lev's father), her parents, grandparents and their whole paraputch could surely cross between worlds. Or perhaps not?

His grandmother lived at the other end of the village. This other end lay a little higher up the hill, and because 'higher' always meant better, the villagers at the top end felt superior. The most northerly part of the country was no different to the big cities: those living higher up were better able to defend themselves from an attack, had fresher air and a nicer view. The bottom, as everyone knew, was where the murky sediment settled, be it people or wine.

Lev's mother would have preferred to have more streets or, even better, whole villages between her and Bunica. At least they lived far enough apart to have to put an extra layer on to visit. When you go to see your in-laws, you should have to put a coat on, as Lis liked to say.

They would probably never admit it, but Lev suspected that the two women liked each other. Even if they didn't, they had at least grown used to each other over the years. His grandmother might emphasise her superiority (the position of her house, her life experience, her nationality), and on such occasions Lis's face would harden, but when it really mattered they could rely on one another.

Bunica praised Lev's mother as little as possible. When she did, she would say: Your mother has golden hands. And it was true. Lis could sew, knit, embroider, and when she decorated cakes or dyed eggs with onion skins, people were amazed by her care and artistry. Lis, in turn, had to acknowledge that Bunica gave good advice in difficult situations. In fact, she gave good advice even before you knew you were in difficulties. She kept the source of her knowledge to herself. Once, when Lev was still at school, she had given him a warning. In the not-too-distant future, she said, someone would come to his classroom and take him to the headmaster's office, but the headmaster would leave at once. The two gentlemen sitting there would, very politely, ask to speak to him – though only one of them would speak; the other would practise his staring. The one who spoke would say: This gentleman would like to know… prefacing all kinds of questions this way, as if the other man was mute or simply too important to open his own mouth. Lev wasn't to be alarmed, but to every question he should reply: I don't know. And if he noticed a waning in politeness, he should ask to be taken back to his classroom. If they ignored his request, he was to say that he'd tell his brothers about this conversation and to give them his brothers' names.

When he asked who these gentlemen were and what they wanted with him, his grandmother said it was better if he didn't know.

How would he recognise them?

By their grey suits, their fine leather shoes.

And so Lev had not been surprised to encounter them in the headmaster's office a few weeks after that conversation.

There were certain things you had to know about Bunica:

She had wanted to be a dancer.

She had married the man she loved.

She had been robbed.

Bunica was seventeen when she and her husband came home after the birth of their first child to find the house had been emptied.

'They took everything from us,' she said. And as if people wouldn't understand what that meant, she repeated, 'Everything.' And if that, too, was not enough, she listed the items they had lost. Bunica was seventeen, a new mother, and she had nothing. No pots and pans, no cutlery, no cushions and blankets, no bedclothes, no lamps; she had no comb, no clothes. All they had left were a few sticks of furniture.

The couple had to buy everything again, second hand. Neighbours donated, friends and family collected. That business brought guilt and grievances – her husband's parents only gave their son the coat they swept the street in. But he was handsome even in this threadbare coat, said Bunica. His photograph in the ancestors' gallery showed off an impressive moustache, next to the pictures of her sons: Lev's father, who had been killed in a landslip, and Lev's uncle, who worked on the shores of the Black Sea (both had the same self-assured, defiant look in their eyes), and when Bunica uttered the word 'handsome' her posture shifted, as if he was standing beside her. The marriage had been happy, she had given him what he wanted when he wanted it – and as a result, she'd had her womb 'scraped', as she called it, several times.

Perhaps, thought Lev, the roots of her unease and restlessness lay in this early experience. Perhaps she had learned then that in an emergency, she could rely only on herself. And perhaps that was why this room dedicated to the past was only used to display things she owned, remaining forever uninhabited in this strange and unignorable way.

Rain grazed the windows; a candle burned on the windowsill. Hard to make out the colours of the woven wall hanging. The crystal was displayed in the vitrine: water carafe, wine carafe, schnapps carafe, water glasses, wine glasses, schnapps glasses, liqueur glasses, dessert plates, vases and ashtray. All painstakingly acquired over the years, and never used. In the open side compartments of the vitrine stood porcelain figurines, painted wooden platters and earthenware jugs. Dolls in Romanian national dress lined the back of the sofa. Icons hung beside window and door.

The startled sofa creased reluctantly, and Lev realised he had been holding his breath as he entered the room. He had long since stopped believing in ghosts, but still preferred the kitchen, where saucepans stood around, clouds of flour flew up and, on warm days, cats waited at the open door, hoping for scraps.

His grandmother set a bottle of soda water and some raspberry syrup on the table, then sat down with a gesture indicating the extent of her sacrifice. Lev could feel the dolls' eyes on the back of his neck.

Getting straight to the point, Bunica said she had heard that the brother and sister from the guesthouse, with whom Lev and Kato had been associating for some years, were being watched and were heading for trouble, at the very highest level.

'You mean Milena and Camil?'

The hope that it wasn't was unrealistic, but he asked anyway.

Streaks of rain robbed the room of almost all light. Bunica nodded, looking as if she had frozen solid, as if the tiniest movement could catapult her back into her usual orbit. Lev picked up a doll; its eyelids clacked shut.

Camil needed to shut up, and she really meant it, he mustn't so much as whistle in church. As for Lev himself (he guessed what she was about to say) – well, in her view it would be wise to stop seeing these people.

He couldn't do that, said Lev.

Bunica looked at the flickering candle on the windowsill.

'Then at least be careful. It isn't as though…'

'I know.'

'You have your grandfather to thank for that.'

The stress on the word 'your' marked the distance between her and Lis's family. The objection was not new in itself.

Since Ferry had fled, they all had him to thank.

Another tool was missing, said Imre by way of greeting. The vices had been delivered the day before, and someone had walked off with a whole bloody vice.

It was probably in a locker somewhere, Lev suspected. No one could spirit a vice away just like that.

He'd had the lockers searched, Imre replied. The vice was gone.

He shook his head when Imre offered schnapps.

Imre shrugged and drained both glasses. He lowered his hand slowly, went to the cabinet and put the glasses back. Imre still had a forest-floor tread, elastic, loping, you never heard him coming. He was patient and generous – up to a point. His instincts told him when he needed to act, and when he could let things take their course. The men respected him. He could distinguish all types of wood by consistency and smell, the way others knew wine. He spoke four languages – Hungarian, Romanian, Ukrainian and German – complete with nuance, irony, humour and imagery, as far as Lev could tell from his own German and Romanian. Imre could read Russian as well, if not speak it, thanks to his origins. He was born in Czernowitz, in the year they decapitated the Lenin statue outside the German Theatre. He said that the place he came from now existed only in literature.

It wasn't lack of respect that made the men steal. It was the same in every business, every industry. If tar was delivered, someone would siphon a little off to tar their driveway. If bricks were delivered, someone would happen to need some for their house just then. If new vices arrived, someone would think: I could do with one of those. Theft was a form of resistance. And this was entirely understandable, given that everything belonged to everyone.

Imre's office window gave onto the production hall. The saws were silent; the only work today was outside in the timber yard, where a load of beechwood was arriving. Through the walls, through the glass, Lev picked up the aroma of the wood, warm, sweetish, a little acidic. Sawdust lay everywhere, on machines, tools, furniture, on shoes and clothes.

'It would have been his birthday today,' said Imre. He was smoking, and smoke escaped from his mouth when he spoke.

How could Lev have forgotten? He had been born in the same year, the same month as Imre's son. He should have thought, should have realised: the morning schnapps, the poetry book open on the table. 'Soon / heaven grows / beneath the grass / your dreams fall / into nowhere. / Still…'

His friend didn't need an extra place setting.

The dead were always at his table.

Imre had not been easy to convince. But he pulled up at the crossroads at the agreed time. Kato had brought her folder and a rucksack. Since the death of her father, she had spent weeks at a time staying with Camil and Milena, helping to serve the customers, drawing, painting. And although she undertook her studies with her usual enthusiasm, to Lev she sometimes seemed lost.

The roads through many of the Iza's tributary valleys were unpaved. The only way to discover the depth of the flooded potholes was to drive through them. But Imre was a cautious driver. Nothing threw him, neither an old woman shouldering her lamb through the village, nor the cyclists moving infinitely slowly. Having registered his preoccupation, Kato made no attempt to chat. Imre had the same sense for Kato's moods. From the beginning, the familiarity between them had surprised Lev.

The rain started again as they drove up into the mountains, flattening grass, driving people indoors. The wipers struggled to keep up. Imre switched the engine off, letting the car coast to the side of the road. Kato opened the door for a boy walking downhill with a piece of cardboard over his head, and the boy got into the back seat with her. They waited for the deluge to pass.

Lev was sure that, normally, Imre would have offered to drive the boy home, but he stayed quiet when the latter thanked them and climbed out. He stirred only when Kato put a tentative hand on his shoulder.

Had it been right to talk Imre into this trip?

Lev hadn't wanted to leave him alone on this day.

Besides, that weekend only cars with odd-numbered plates were allowed on the roads. Imre's car was odd-numbered.

Milena was plucking her eyebrows. She didn't turn around, just angled the mirror to catch the guests' reflection as they entered.

'Come on in,' she said, sounding a little stiff because her eyebrows were raised.

Kato, Imre and Lev stepped into the bar room, which

was clean and tidy, with woven cloths on the tables, ashtrays and candles that weren't lit. Milena stood under a lamp, light pouring onto her face and shoulders, while the rest of the room lay in half-darkness. As always, Lev felt comfortable at once, perhaps because it was such an unlikely place. A guesthouse in the mountains, in a village that might have been significant once. From outside, little distinguished it from the other wooden houses, no name, no sign, nothing to say it was a guesthouse at all. When you went inside, an improbable depth was revealed – dark wooden tables, chairs, bar, barstools, wall hangings. However short supplies were, Milena always had wine, homemade schnapps and some kind of food to offer.

'I brought a friend,' said Lev.

'I can see that.'

'Good afternoon,' said Imre. Somehow, he didn't sound convincing.

Lev placed a packet of sugar on the bar. In all the time they had known each other, he had never come without a gift.

Two locals walked in and asked for drinks. Milena sent the men away, saying they were closed.

They were never closed on Fridays, one objected.

'We are now,' Milena told him. 'Come back later.'

Seeing there was nothing to be done, they gave up.

'You're sending customers away?' Lev asked.

'It isn't every day you bring me a friend.'

While Lev considered the odd emphasis she had given to the word 'friend', Kato asked after Camil. Her brother was outside, Milena said. Through the window, they saw Camil driving two bony-flanked horses into the yard. Kato ran out despite the rain and kissed him. He wrapped his arms around her, lifting her off the ground. When Camil walked into the bar room and saw Imre, his left eye twitched.

'Cum eşti, ce faci?'

'Fac supa de clopot.'

If you asked Camil how he was, what he was doing, he'd say he was making soup out of bells. Kato couldn't stand it when he used that expression. But Camil said that one day the church bells would ring for each of them.

With a tilt of his head, Lev let Camil know that he wanted to speak to him alone. Camil took the towel his sister handed him and stepped out into the back courtyard, under the eaves. Lev passed on his grandmother's warning. He took a few cautious detours around the information, like someone covering his tracks. Camil had met Bunica only once, but that was enough to take what she said seriously.

Rain dripped from Camil's hair. He was fourteen years older than Lev, a tall, hulking man with a warmth in his eyes like the smouldering of small fires. No one knew exactly what Camil did. He could get hold of anything, identity papers, documents, and, when Lev was doing his military service, he had procured a driver's licence from God knows where for the tunnel's civil engineer. Lev handed over the licence, and not long afterwards was released from the tunnel – even managing to get a transfer for another young soldier he had taken under his wing.

Camil dried his hair without speaking. Lev joined him in this silence, as if their conversation continued there. He liked

Camil, was grateful to him. But a distance remained that they couldn't bridge and perhaps didn't want to.

He made an effort, for Kato's sake.

She was blackening a section of paper with charcoal.

Her posture over the drawing was a turning away and a turning towards; escape. No one knew better than Lev how much she needed that escape. Camil got hold of paints and paper, he praised, he criticised. Lev didn't speak that language. A picture was beautiful, or it wasn't. He had no words for what lay between.

In the evening, the bar room was nicely full. The men Milena had turned away came back, other customers arrived from the village and surrounding area. Drink was taken, card games were played. When the news came on, Milena turned the radio down, though not quite off. That would have been too dramatic a gesture.

At around ten o'clock, Imre hinted that it was about time to leave.

Milena exchanged a look with her brother.

'You can't go without trying my schnapps,' Camil told him.

When they had both drained their glasses, Camil poured them another.

'One's enough,' Imre protested.

'Did you like it or not?'

He had to drive, Imre objected.

Important, then, to fortify yourself for the journey, said Camil. All objections were dismissed, and while the alcohol took effect on Imre, Camil seemed to feel nothing at all. Lev had been looking all evening for signs that Bunica's warning had unsettled him. If it had, he hid it well. Kato didn't seem much interested in the drinking game, but Milena didn't take her eyes off the pair.

Soon, there was no further need of persuasion techniques.

No one was driving anywhere that evening.

When the last customers had gone, Milena pushed the tables against the walls and invited Imre to dance. Lev danced with Kato. It was a fast song; they whirled. Kato laughed. Then she gave him a questioning look. It had been a while since he visited her; he blamed work, and often he would stay at the sawmill until late evening. Not because Imre expected it, but because he enjoyed the work. He'd never had plans for a career. From summers in the forest, he knew he liked working with wood and found office work easy. But if Imre hadn't asked him to help out in the sawmill when he returned from military service, who knows what path he would have taken.

You do too much waiting, his mother said. It was true, and it wasn't. Like everyone else, he was waiting for this time to end. In the mornings, he waited to see if Lis or Bunica needed anything. He joined the queue to wait for butter or bread. He waited for spring, for the rain, for an end to his loneliness.

And Kato? Sometimes she seemed happy, almost carefree. And then hesitant, doubtful. But, unlike him, she had something that drove her, fulfilled her, a talent that was obvious to everyone. Even her father seemed to have realised it in the end, requesting a picture of his beehives long after he'd stopped keeping bees. Lavishly late.

'Milena likes him,' said Kato.

'She does?'

She gave him an amused look.

'How can you not notice?'

Camil was smoking, leaning on the bar, Milena and Imre barely moving, but Lev didn't look at them; all he saw were light grey eyes and three moles – a line that continued, he knew, across throat, breast, down to her belly.

Lev didn't mind spending the night. Kato would stay until the first of May, and if Imre was late for work tomorrow, then Lev could be too. The sofa had been set up for him, and the clouded mirror by the door watched him pulling random books off the shelves. A living room was the extension of a body – someone letting you step into their innermost self. Lev was tired, but he couldn't sleep. Outside the window, water cascaded from the guttering onto the tarmac.

When he passed Milena's room on the way back from the toilet, he heard voices inside, open-mouthed breathing, half-stifled laughter. The bedhead knocked against the wall, sheets and pillows rustled. He had an image of Milena's back, the indentations of her spine, her bare white arms. And Imre? He must be underneath, or the noises would be different, harder, faster; his face was probably relaxed, his eyes half closed.

There were days when his friend submerged, was stubbornly silent. They were followed by periods of action when nothing was too risky: freeing a piece of wood jammed in a machine, felling trees in impassable places, picking fights with everyone and everything. Imre kept death near, as if it would bring him closer to his son. Lev found it hard to accept such grief. He'd hoped it would dissipate, lessen over time, but it was too great.

He lingered by Milena's door, incapable of going past, and listened to the two of them breathing, noises translating themselves into images, until Imre came.

She had wanted him at first sight, thought Lev.

Back on the sofa, he thought of Astrid. Lust and guilt stirred in him. Why didn't they move in together, Astrid had asked, abruptly making him aware that he couldn't imagine it. Astrid belonged to Sighişoara, and the town where his mother and grandfather had grown up was completely separate from his life in the village. Impossible to mix these two lives.

She had been sitting at his grandfather's kitchen table one afternoon, and Ferry soon found some pretext to disappear into his workshop, leaving them in a tense silence. Lev was angry at this obvious matchmaking attempt, considered leaving at once, but then realised that, against expectations, he liked her. She was a nursery school teacher with light blonde hair, almost white eyelashes and an attentive, inviting way of asking questions and listening that made her easy to trust.

They went for walks, to the cinema, and everything was unequivocal in a way he had never known before. He admired how honest, sensual and direct she was. When he told her that, she laughed. He told her often. He wanted her to know how beautiful she was in his eyes, how much he desired her.

'You must be in love,' she said.

It was the truth, he answered.

'You being in love, or me being beautiful?'

'Both.'

Astrid got hold of the pill from Germany. Friends brought supplies over the border, sewn into coat seams. Lev liked the way she could surrender herself, her body responding to his touch. She had shown him what mattered to her: delay, certainty, a feeling of safety.

He felt comfortable in her family, which was calmer than his own; their togetherness was natural, self-evident. His mother was pleased when Astrid came to visit, baking and laying the table, and it was a huge effort for Lev to ignore the commitment these visits implied. She was astute enough to see it and demanded a decision, but he couldn't see why. Weren't things good as they were? Astrid pressed for the next step, and her idea of a new start began to feel like an ending.

He didn't reveal his doubt. He was evasive, holding back the words he should have spoken. One evening he drove all the way to her house, threw pebbles at the window and called her down to the front door, but the words he had planned to say stuck in his throat. Astrid stood barefoot in her nightshirt before him. They looked at one another in silence; he wrestled with himself and then left, taking all he had to say with him.

Such hesitancy had consequences, and she made that abundantly clear. The last time he came to collect her, she wasn't at home, or at least pretended not to be. The pebbles on her window produced no echo, no footsteps in the stairwell, no front door opening. He would bring her flowers, books, whatever she wanted, until she took him back. He longed to be in Astrid's bed, and he pressed himself into the sofa until he had calmed down.

The next morning, Imre and Lev drove straight to work. Kato stayed in the mountains. She kissed him goodbye, as always, on the lips.

'Call when you want me to come and get you,' he said.

Camil walked them to the car, which he had never done before, and gave him a farewell hug. Lev watched his figure in the wing mirror until they rounded the first bend.

They said nothing all the way back. The engine and the rhythm of the wipers were the only sounds. Lev guessed what his friend was thinking about, grinned, and hurriedly ran a hand over his face, but Imre had already registered the grin. From that moment, if not before, Imre knew that Lev knew.

In the sawmill, the machines stood silent. The eternally vibrating floor was still. No one was in the timber yard, on the belts or at the saws. The silence in the high-ceilinged space, open at one side, felt like a vision of reality. Everything was supposed to move constantly forwards into a golden future, but the crack between slogans and the real world gaped ever wider.

Imre summoned the foreman, Yakob.

Yakob said it had not been clear what to do with the delivery of wood. The workers had gone home.

Imre didn't waste another word. He kept his cool with Yakob – which had something to do with the number tattooed on Yakob's forearm.

When Lev wondered at how calmly he had accepted the stoppage, Imre said more had been lost at Mohács. Which was one way of saying: things could be worse.

They spent the rest of the day going through papers, sorting orders, bills, delivery slips, sick notes, changes in legislation, while Yakob ran saw blades through the tooth setter. When they were finished, Imre walked Lev to the exit.

'When will you see her again?'

'Tomorrow,' said Imre, without hesitation.

Lev pulled his hood up and stepped out into the rain. When he turned around, he saw Imre lighting a cigarette. The match lit up his face, lit up a smile.

At an Orthodox service, you cross yourself constantly. As you walk in and kiss the icons, during the psalms, before the singing, after the singing, when you pray, when the priest prays. Always.

People came and went, lighting candles (on the chandelier for the living; in the sand for the dead), kneeling; children ran around, coins clanged into coffers. Not many stayed for the duration, which even on a normal Sunday could stretch to two or three hours. A few older women sat on the fringes, bolt upright; crossing legs was frowned upon. Bunica stood. Standing, she showed Him that she was serious, and by crossing herself that her whole body was praying, not just her mind.

Lev had her to thank for being allowed in at all, and even permitted to take communion. He didn't know how she had arranged it; Protestants, like Catholics, were not admitted. When the priest gave him bread and wine with the spoon, he thought he saw a censorious frown cloud the man's face.

Bunica insisted that, though her youngest grandson had been baptised a Protestant, which of course he couldn't help, he should come to know the Orthodox faith. This had caused arguments, but over the years Lis had stopped resisting, and so Lev attended the Protestant service when he was at Astrid's, as well as the Orthodox church in the village. God, he had decided, would not mind; after all, both religions had the man on the cross. At Christmas he went to the Catholic church with his mother for the annual performance of 'Herod the Great', and sometimes at Easter he went to a Ruthenian service. He was particularly fond of this church, the isolation of the mountain village, and its name – Poienile de sub Munte – not beside or by a mountain, but under it.

The inside of the wooden church was like a ship's hold, the steeple an arrow into the sky. The rhythm of the services was like breathing. The gold-embroidered robes, candles, incense, song, and the alternation between action, stillness and prayer, all gave him a feeling of presentness he found nowhere else. Bunica noted this with a silent satisfaction, as if she had won some kind of competition. Why the German churches had pews was a mystery to her. You don't go to watch, she said, you're not at the cinema or in a university. Lev doubted whether his grandmother had ever been inside a cinema or a university.

Out on the street after the service, Bunica flagged down a man on a horse-drawn cart. Her legs had to ache after standing for hours, but she would never admit it. She used to ride her dust-grey donkey to church, but now he was old, too, and spent all day standing by the sun-warmed wall of the woodshed. And Lev wasn't allowed to pick his grandmother up in the car – one did not drive a car to church.

They settled down on the bed of the cart, spreading newspapers to absorb the wet. Behind them stood crates of empty soda bottles. Lev held the umbrella over the two of them and smoked. Bunica hadn't lingered outside the church as usual; she even snubbed a woman who was heading purposefully towards her, certain to be bringing a wealth of gossip. She said nothing all the way home, though usually she told stories as they travelled somewhere together. Bunica's stories waited in the landscape, inscribed into houses, trees, streams. That was the gate where the Russians shot a man on the first day. (You only had to shoot one man in a village, then everyone obeyed.) That was the hiding place that concealed first a Jew, then a Wehrmacht soldier, then a Saxon, and who knows, maybe a Romanian partisan, too.

She wouldn't ask if he had warned Camil. The things she said were statements, not investigations. And once she'd said them, she could let them go; they were out of her hands. Lev had once asked where she got her knowledge. Knowledge came from the body, the whole body, she said – but regrettably, most people never got beyond their heads.

The cart stopped at Bunica's gate and Lev helped his grandmother down. She usually invited him in for lunch, but today no invitation came; instead, she asked if he'd seen an earthworm.

He thought he'd misheard.

Bunica pushed her headscarf back, pointed at the ground.

'Normally there would be earthworms everywhere.'

Now he came to think of it, she was right.

When Lev looked back from the end of the street, Bunica was still standing at her gate, peering up at the sky.

The first of May fell on a Thursday. Khalil brought him a pigeon to mark the occasion. Lev found it on the rug by his bed. He picked it up; its heart was racing, it was stiff with shock, but it was alive. And uninjured, as far as he could tell. Lev placed it carefully on the windowsill.

Khalil must think him entirely stupid. In all these years, Lev had neither learned to hunt for himself, nor been especially pleased with bird gifts. Khalil's forays had extended recently, and sometimes he wouldn't come home for a whole day or even two. Lis said that cats never belonged to you alone. A cat always had many names, three at least: the one it had at home, the one other people gave it, convinced the cat belonged to them (because it arrived for meals and occasionally slept on bedside rugs and armchairs), and the name it alone knew. That was why they were so aloof. Only those who know your secret name have power over you, Lis said – and Lev hoped that Kato had at least come close when she christened the cat.

They spent Labour Day by the Iza. The previous evening the sky had finally cleared, and now streams and rivers were swollen, the meadows wet. The weather god is on your side, said Anuța, who had joined his family for the day. She went with different people every year. Lev counted: his sister Bredica and her husband Ion, the three children (who had all inherited their mother's thick, dark hair, especially his niece, who looked like a timid animal), his brothers Valea and Dorin, Dorin's wife Silvia, their newborn, his mother, his grandmother, Anuța, and Lev himself. Nine adults, three children, a baby. Another group was setting up camp a few metres away. Everyone was outside today.

Blankets were spread and Valea and Ion took care of the barbecue, fanning the embers, unsuccessfully at first because the wood was damp. Bredica's husband was the only person who enjoyed Valea's company.

Dorin had found this spot. He came here with the lecturers who travelled the country for the 'cultural education of the people' and were mostly greeted with empty halls. Only Lev and Bredica knew what really went on. Dorin's older brother was always off at some meeting or other, called everyone 'comrade', and had lately started wearing a hat instead of a cap – when he was around, Dorin would never admit that the farmers stayed away from those events. Some fictional number of audience members would be recorded, and then the lecturers would go fishing.

Lis asked if anyone knew why the shops were so full. There had been an unusual amount of fruit and vegetables. The townsfolk hadn't even had to queue for milk, Anuța added. No one had an answer, and Valea, the only one who might have known, concentrated on poking the embers.

The cradle was hung on a tree branch. The baby's eyes were open but he couldn't recognise anything yet, Dorin explained. Traditionally babies were swaddled, wrapped in cloth from head to toe. Lev felt the boy's paralysis keenly.

Dorin's wife Silvia looked tired, absentminded. She rocked the cradle with one hand, not looking at the child. She had spoken barely a word since the birth, and the slightest thing could make her cry. On the first family visit after the baby was born, she'd handed him over as if she didn't know what to do with him, and it was Lis who thought of scissors to cut the baby's nails; his cheeks were scratched.

Lev sat with Silvia and tried to start a conversation, which remained one-sided until Dorin called him over.

'Can't you see she's tired?'

'Can't you see she's not well?' Lev shot back.

'She's exhausted, that's all.'

This woman didn't seem exhausted.

Lev knew that inward look.

'Look after her,' said Lev. 'Take some of the work from her.'

What was he trying to say, his brother asked, did Lev want him to get busy in the kitchen, or what. His tone didn't fit his gestures. He seemed tense; his brother's usually open, approachable face had fallen in.

'That would be a start,' said Lev, unmoved.

Bunica perched on a rock, peeling potatoes. She could peel off precise snakes of skin with her knife. She needed help to get up.

'Never grow old,' she told the children, who were picking up the peelings and hanging them in the bushes like garlands. 'Age wears heavy clothes.'

Apple trees blossomed in the meadows. The Iza was in restless motion, with a family every twenty or thirty metres along its bank. Lev's niece and his two nephews ran into the water, though their father warned them it was still too cold.

'Come in!' they urged Lev.

Lev rolled up his trouser legs and waded into the river, splashing them as if by accident. He soon escaped onto a rock. The children didn't seem to feel the cold. They built a dam for which Lev hauled rocks, watched fish that appeared only when they were still and quiet, tried to create a sandy beach at the water's edge, looked for glittering stones, claiming they were silver. Then his niece got cold and he picked her up, staying in the shallows until the cold became a stabbing pain in his feet. Eventually he stopped thinking about Kato (he had saved his petrol ration in case she wanted him to collect her), or the argument with Astrid; he stopped thinking of the chaos in the sawmill, of anything at all.

They ate barbecued meat, potatoes and cabbage salad, with cake for dessert and chocolate from Ferry's latest parcel. After the meal, Bunica and Anuța washed the plates in the river. At the children's insistence, Bredica began to tell a story. Lev listened with half an ear: twelve brothers had been turned into black horses, and their sister rescued them from a floating mountain.

Lis was reading on a blanket in the grass, stretched out on her back, the book close to her face. Tree shadows drifted over the book's cover; her face, deeply shadowed, wore an expression of such contentment that Lev couldn't look away. Only she could be absorbed in a book on an afternoon like this, surrounded by conversation and stories. How did she find rest here? How did she live in the middle of this family, an eternal stranger after more than twenty years? She got on with most of the neighbours, had a few friends. Was it enough? Did she miss her father? Life in town? His mother seemed to have found refuge here, though from what or whom, Lev didn't know.

The tale of the floating mountain ended with the siblings being given a horse that could find the greatest treasures in the land. Lev's nephews sat reverently on the blanket; his niece was sucking a strand of her mother's hair. Bredica finished by saying that she would like a horse like that. 'Then I wouldn't have to cook, or do laundry, or tell you stories every day.'

The children laughed, and Bredica got up and went to sit behind Dorin's wife. She rubbed her shoulders, massaged her neck, her touch fluid and casual.

Silvia closed her eyes, lowered her hand.

Now the wind rocked the cradle.

Now the baby's eyes closed, too.

Kato was waiting on the bench by the gate. He wanted to start asking how she had spent the holiday, how she got back to the village, but Lis, who was quicker to grasp the situation, gave him a sign and invited her in. In his room, Kato flopped onto the bed. As he closed the door behind his mother, who had brought them a plate of cake, a sense of foreboding came over him, but he said nothing, waiting for her to tell him herself.

She kicked off her shoes, leaned back, Khalil rubbed against her, and it was almost like the old days. They had spent whole afternoons on his bed, and the memory brought a smile that Lev managed to suppress just in time.

'Camil has gone,' said Kato. 'He disappeared yesterday.'

He must have set off early because he wasn't there when she woke. One of the horses was missing, a rucksack and a few items of clothing, as far as she and Milena could judge. In the days beforehand he'd been strange, dismissive, stalking about as if trying to spoil everyone's fun, he'd even made a disparaging comment about one of her drawings.

'That doesn't sound like Camil,' said Lev.

She stroked the cat, avoided looking at him.

He felt a rush of guilt. He had warned Camil, which made him part of this disappearance, and he was afraid that Kato guessed as much. But Lev couldn't tell her anything; she would badger his grandmother, and Bunica would not reveal her source.

Imre had dropped by, she said, and various friends over the course of the day. Conversations took place among the fruit trees, with Milena hoping someone had heard something or been privy to her brother's plans. They had to be careful. It was said that one in five people would betray you.

He hadn't even left a note or a letter, for his sister or Kato. She ate some of Lis's cake, but tears ran down her cheeks as she chewed. Lev gently took the plate from her hand, sat down and gave her a hug. Khalil moved to the foot of the bed; he had never been one for excessive sadness. As her sobs ebbed away, Lev heard himself saying that Camil would come back soon. He said it to her, and for himself, and it felt as if he had icicles in his mouth.

'Can I stay?'

'Always. As long as you want.'

They lay down. Her hair tickled him, his arm went numb, but he didn't release the embrace. Kato fell into a restless sleep, and soon he nodded off, too. In his dreams he saw Camil in a car, in the forest, in a cellar. He dreamed of a lake with a mountain floating in it. The mountain turned slowly on its axis, and he and Kato stood on the shore, not knowing how to get across.

Just before midnight, Khalil wanted to go out. Lev detached himself cautiously from Kato and went into the main room to open the front door for the cat. What he saw could have been another dream: a candle was burning on the table, and Bunica and Lis sat facing one another in silence, his grandmother's posture strangely lopsided, as if she was about to leave.

Bunica said she'd heard something when she was taking the radio out into the maize, you know, for the wild boar. It had been accidentally tuned to Radio Europa Liberă România. She spoke in barely more than a whisper, and the word 'accidentally' came with a meaningful look. Lis didn't seem surprised; Bunica had clearly shared the news already.

There had been an accident in a nuclear power station near Kiev. The Russians weren't giving out any specific information, probably not even to their own population. Other countries had known for three days. But unfortunately, she had only been back out to the maize this evening, because of the rain, and only late, because her neighbour…

'What else did you hear?' Lev interrupted.

'A reactor exploded. The poison it released has no colour or scent. It spreads through the air, on the wind…' She faltered. 'In the rain.'

It had been raining for days, thought Lev, and today, the children in the river. The cold of the water, silver stones, sand. He felt his legs going numb, pulled the chair towards him. Why hadn't they been informed? Why didn't countries work together? What did borders even mean in a case like this?

Bunica and Lis were also lost in thought. All at once, his grandmother seemed very tired. He stretched an arm across the table, and Bunica looked at his hand and then took it, with some delay. Lis held out a hand as well.

'It is how it's always been,' she said. 'Like a theatre where they only ever put on one play. But people don't tire of watching it. They go to the performance, suffer, hope, and applaud when the great catastrophe is averted in the nick of time.'

And the worst thing, said Bunica, was when people imagined they were learning something. When they thought that times were getting better and they were getting cleverer. Everything repeated, everything returned, just with a different face.

Lev tried to fathom the implications of this news; he thought of Kato asleep in his room, of Camil's disappearance, and felt like he had as a child, walking into Bunica's parlour. If something had to be fetched, his brothers would send him – he wasn't scared, was he? In the still, twilit room, the furniture loomed like stone giants and, for fear that something might grab him by the shoulder, he didn't breathe.

Why had holding his breath been so important?

Why did it stop the ghosts from hurting you?

That's easy, he heard his sister's voice saying.

People who don't breathe are already dead.

The next day, it was on the Romanian news as well: there had been an accident at the Lenin Nuclear Power Station, not far from Kiev. Children would be given iodine tablets at school. Unnecessary time outdoors was to be avoided. Picking mushrooms was not advisable. Fruit and vegetables should be washed thoroughly, and people should stop drinking milk. Otherwise, there was no danger to the population.

Prin pădure trece-mi-oi
Frunză verde ciunta-mi-oi
Şi pe vale şi pe grui

Five

Nothing.

Dammit.

He could see nothing.

The windscreen was all but useless. He could make out the occasional feature only when Kato wiped the glass with a rag soaked in schnapps. Were the roads mapped out in his memory? Was he trusting to luck? In his right mind? When they stopped to get their bearings, all that lay beneath the low, snow-drifting sky were more hills.

Kato soaked the rag in schnapps, got out, wiped the windscreen. Shapes appeared through the peephole, outlines, grey on grey, white on white, then cold fingers of ice closed the circle again. For a few seconds, Lev drove into nothingness. Swore.

'How much is left?'

'There's enough,' she replied, in a slightly vague tone that told him she too had doubts.

No other people, no cars in sight; they were the only ones mad enough to be out in this weather. A while later, some houses came into view. Kato let out a delighted cry of 'mişto!' and took a swig from the bottle. Lev slowed even further, if that was possible, and they stared at forbidding, abandoned-looking fences and yards until a light appeared.

A faint ribbon, but light all the same.

Lev walked ahead and realised to his surprise that they had stumbled across an inn. Candles were burning on the tables. The flames guttered and righted themselves as Kato shut the door. Three men and a woman were gathered around a radio. The woman turned, casually appraising them. The warmth of the room kept Lev rooted in the doorway. Snow was melting in Kato's hair; she too stood, eyes fixed on the scene. Whenever the radio played a song by Maria Tănase, this happened: people fell silent, some closed their eyes, others stared into space, head propped on one hand as a part of them turned inward, was lost or gathered itself.

Her voice was rough, not classically beautiful, but she could be tender or grand, could sing of love or drinking, and her songs spanned the Maramureş, Transylvania, all the way down to Wallachia. She had been banned from performing and it was forbidden to play her music – which was effective, evidently. The song had finished and only a crackle hung in the air, but the group stayed motionless by the radio. Lev and Kato remained at the door, incapable of disturbing the tableau.

This silence, thought Lev, came from the notes and was still telling their story; it was replete and full and had to dissipate, like smoke.

The woman broke the spell.

'What do you want here?'

It didn't sound hostile.

Guilt: what was it, really?

There was no guilt, just a series of decisions.

Lev had leave from the military and on his first evening home, drove his grandfather's car over to her house. Before he could even get out, he saw Kato's slender figure running down the path, passing so close to the pear tree that she set the swing in motion, and climbing over the low fence, which bowed to the ground in some places as if staggering. The passenger door was flung open, Kato held a bottle out to him and cried, Drive! When he asked where to, her reply was oriunde – wherever.

They drove up into the mountains, bend after bend, despite the snow that had begun to fall, drinking schnapps until they felt warm and no longer knew where they were.

'There's no way you can go back now,' the woman told them with a glance out of the window. 'Leave in the morning, if you can see anything.'

'But I have to,' Kato said softly.

'You don't have to do anything, sweetheart. Or shall we light a candle in your memory tomorrow?'

Milena, that was her name, placed bowls of vegetable soup in front of them. She didn't offer schnapps, because, she said, the pair of them already smelled like her bar room on the feast of the Assumption.

Two of the men said their goodbyes. Milena introduced the one who stayed as her brother. Camil had longish hair and a powerful frame and might have been around thirty. He looked melancholy. As if he'd just been told about an accident. And he had a nervous affliction: his left eyelid twitched.

In an ice-cold room on the upper floor, the sofa bed was pulled out for them. Lev hesitated for a moment, since it was a double. Was that a problem, Milena asked innocently, but without waiting for an answer.

A large bookcase, pictures on the walls. Hemp cloths hung over the back of a chair. Kato lifted them to her face, breathed in, then flopped onto the sofa bed, still fully dressed. Lev washed at the washstand, took off shoes and trousers and got under the covers, with some difficulty at first as Kato made no effort to make room. Then she did the same, washed and undressed. He felt cold legs sliding between his own.

With his first pay packet from the forest, he had bought her shoes. Kato stared at them, not moving, not speaking. Then at last, she said: Shoes.

Only when he said shoes as well, as if the word had only now entered both their vocabularies, had she kicked off her old shoes and put on the new ones, carefully, as if they were made of glass, tying the laces in bows slowly, like a child – she still did that. She walked a few steps, watching out for any stones, quickened her pace, and finally twisted down to the ground to feel the leather. She stretched her legs out, knocked the toes of her shoes together, leapt up and started running, as if it were the shoes themselves setting the pace. One leg drew an arc through the air, then the other, and in between came moments when both legs were airborne and Kato was weightless.

She had never said thank you.

Nor did she have to.

He would hand over his gifts without fuss (an exercise book, a cup, fine-meshed tights, which she had never worn) and change the subject at once. Sometimes he hid them, so Kato would find them a while later. They never talked about it, but he knew when she had found something from the joy of the discovery stored in her face. He could not get enough of her face, which could change in a flash from exuberant to thoughtful, serious to euphoric. Her expression kept an undertone of aloofness, something that remained foreign to him, even though he knew her face better than any other. She was almost as tall as him now, her arms and legs had grown lanky, but her eyes had not changed. The clear, grey light in them, curiosity, cleverness, intransigence.

He stretched out an arm and Kato laid her head on it.

It was light enough to see furniture and books, to vaguely make out her silhouette under the covers. Kato turned over to face him and sighed. Her breath was on his neck, her legs on his; now, thought Lev, now, and turned to her. He began to pester her tenderly, restlessly. His hand stroked her neck, her shoulders, he kissed cheeks and eyelids. His tongue parted her lips. In her mouth, damp, bitter sweetness, like the taste of green hazelnuts. She let it happen, didn't back away, and that emboldened him. He rolled onto her, taking care not to let cold air under the covers, felt her breasts, which he had seen so often down at the river, felt her hips, the warmth of her belly. He pressed himself against her, groaned.

'Lev… Lev!'

The next morning was bright, the sky unclouded. Lev felt exposed; he closed his eyes against the light in the hope that his whole body might disappear behind the lids. Silence snagged against their table. The bar room smelled of cold smoke. Camil sat at the window, watching birds through a pair of binoculars. Milena gave them polenta with milk, which they ate hungrily.

Not watching Kato that morning was an art. Not looking as they dressed; not noticing as she traced the blooms of ice on the window with her fingers and looked at herself in the cloudy mirror by the door; letting her use the bathroom first with a polite gesture; and gazing subtly past her at the breakfast table, squinting to take everything in, the swept floor, the faded pictures on the walls, while leaving her face out of focus.

Milena poured coffee, stopped at their table with evident bewilderment and asked if they'd swallowed their tongues. Both hastily thanked her. Then Kato asked what Camil was doing over there. It was the first full sentence she had uttered that morning.

Her brother, Milena informed them, was studying the blackbirds.

When no one responded, Camil spoke up. His voice was deep, filling the room, breaking mid-sentence into a huskiness that was somehow compelling. He cut an impressive figure, but had a spiritual air about him.

Camil said that blackbirds were the most unobtrusive of creatures, but they sang more beautifully than any nightingale. He was trying to work out how they communicated, was noting down their songs.

Kato, who had got up from her seat, took the binoculars and recoiled.

Camil laughed and showed her how to adjust the focus.

Suddenly, Kato and Camil were close.

Perhaps that was why Lev couldn't like him unreservedly.

Kato, who had joined in the squinting game, did not spare him on the way home. As soon as the inside of the car had warmed up and they were back on familiar roads, she brought it up. Her tongue brushed softly against her teeth, as always when she was tired or agitated.

'Listen Lev, I'm not angry with you.'

Some bends required real concentration.

'It was probably about time – I've been thinking about it for a while. You too?'

A nod couldn't hurt, and he threw one carelessly into his otherwise diligent driving.

'You know, whatever might take the place of what we already have, couldn't be nearly as good.'

'You can't know that if we don't try.'

What would happen if they didn't find the courage to go one step further now?

'You must know how much you mean to me.'

'Really?' he asked, a little too loudly. 'Tell me, because I don't. I just know I think about you, I think about you all the time when I'm working in that hellhole.'

She took his hand, which reluctantly left the gearstick.

'Why don't you tell me about it?' she asked.

Lev thought about the tunnel, the cold, the barracks. He didn't want to be pitied.

'I can't risk it.' Something in her voice forced him to look at her. 'You're the only friend I have.'

'It would work out,' he said quietly.

It hurt so much that she didn't believe it.

'It's bad with my father when he's out of work. He sits around the house from morning till night, then suddenly disappears for days at a time.'

'Is that his bottle?'

'That *was* his bottle,' said Kato, picking it up from the footwell. Only a dribble remained.

They grinned at each other.

'You're away, and I'm here.' (At 'here' she gestured vaguely.) 'You'll meet a woman, you probably already have, how else did you learn to kiss like that.'

'Well, at least there's that.'

'What?'

'At least you think I'm a good kisser.'

They laughed. Kato shot him a look of relief.

The hills and streets of their village gradually assembled themselves from the sparse lines ahead. When they reached her house, Kato threw the car door open before they had even stopped. A scrape, a creak announced the opening of the front door. Kato's mind was already in the house, with her father, with the explanation of where she had been. Lev wanted to say something to lift the sadness he had seen in her so often lately.

But what?

Everyone fell in when the military called. Some, like Lev, were eighteen, others a fair bit older, having only been drafted when they finished their education.

No one knew where they were headed. Like most, Lev had just one suitcase. Inside: underwear, something to eat. His mother had packed far too much. His sister Bredica had given him a talisman from the children, a plastic owl with a keyring attached to it. His grandmother advised him not to stand out, to keep quiet when expected to and speak when required, and then he would disappear into the crowd. In these situations, disappearing was important. Dorin gave him a penknife. Valea said goodbye as if he was off to the fields or the forest – in other words, not at all.

The train journey took all night. When it was a journey. Sometimes they stopped to let another train overtake. No one cared if they were hungry or thirsty. They didn't arrive until morning, and Lev recognised the flat land, the horizon low as if drawn with a steady hand.

Someone said Banat.

Someone said Reşiţa!

They went straight from the station to the barracks, and he got a first, fleeting impression of the city. Blocks of flats and houses without ornament, without wooden gables or benches set into the wall outside the gates. Smoke blue, apple green, ochre yellow. Industry filled the hillsides with its chimneys, cooling towers and warehouses. He could hear a droning, a mechanical hum. The sight filled Lev with a gloom that mingled with his disquiet, his feverish tiredness.

What kind of city was this? It had a river, at least – the Bârzava.

More waiting in the barracks. His name was called and sounded unfamiliar, like a question. A question he answered with his whole body, with his presence. He felt no embarrassment at being naked. He was strong from the logging work of summer. His clothes were stuffed into a sack, and the sack was sewn up and labelled with his name. Then his head was shaved. The trousers of his uniform were too short, as were the sleeves of the jacket, and no one asked his size before handing him a pair of shoes, either. They began to swap; finding the right shoes took longest. Eventually, he got some that were more worn than his original pair, but fitted. The underpants were the only things he could not come to terms with. They were scratchy and fastened with a crude string.

Nothing but drills for weeks. They had to muster for roll call straight after breakfast, and again morning and afternoon for military drills. Target practice took place in a meadow, fenced off to prevent civilians entering the line of fire.

Lev didn't mind the drills, or the monotonous mealtime readings about Ceauşescu's heroic deeds, as if they were monks in a refectory hearing about God. What got to him was the officers' malice. As a youngest sibling, Lev understood hierarchies: if Valea had a bad day, he took it out on Dorin. Dorin in turn took his mood out on Lev, and Lev was always left to wonder whether that sequence ended with him. His mother couldn't help. Valea and Dorin wouldn't listen to her now; she was to cook for them, but not lay down the law.

They had Sundays off, but on one of the first Sundays they were fetched out of bed in the early morning to dig a ditch. Three metres were marked out for each of them. The earth was hard, their pickaxes hit one stone after another, and anyone who didn't fulfil his quota got no dinner. Lev brought bread and cheese to the man who hadn't dug his metres. A young Serb with homesickness etched on his face.

The children's plastic owl lay under his pillow. It was the first thing he saw when he opened his eyes, the last thing before he closed them. The suitcase Lev kept under the bed became his writing desk, stool – a pledge from another world. Sometimes he slid it out and ran a hand over the underwear that Lis had packed and that, like all the precious things in there, he was not allowed to use. The army-issue underpants tormented him more and more; the scratching became unbearable, the string would loosen during drills, and they would slip and hang around his backside like a rag. Without hesitation, he changed them for a pair brought from home.

A short while later, Lev was pulled out of bed in the night. Two men dragged him into the barrack yard. Darkness hid their faces. The scent of vanilla and a trace of ash hung in the air.

He was made to strip to his underpants.

A shooting star scorched the night in two.

Then the kicking started.

If not for the incident with the underpants, he might have sworn his oath.

After basic training, they were called before the commandant one by one to take the oath. Hand on rifle, eyes on the tricolour, for the fatherland.

He wouldn't swear, said Lev.

The commandant checked that he had not misheard.

Lev said nothing and cast an apparently indifferent glance at the second man, who'd passed him the rifle. A guy in a properly fitting uniform, which he hadn't got by swapping; he gave off a sweetish aroma like pipe tobacco. Vanilla and ash.

Threats followed. They would have him up before the military court in Timişoara if he didn't swear now. Other soldiers were waiting outside, this process was like a conveyor belt. Lev saw the commandant's dismay.

More attempts at verbal intimidation followed.

Lev put down the rifle, repeated that he wouldn't swear.

Now the other man got involved.

What would he swear on, then?

Lev glanced around the room.

A wave of exuberance overtook him.

Either they will hack you to pieces, or you'll get away with it.

'I'll swear on this broom,' he said, pointing to the corner where a broom was leaning next to a bucket.

The door opened; someone asked if everything was alright.

'Yes,' barked the commandant. 'Of course everything's alright!'

The door closed again.

The vanilla man pressed the broom into Lev's hand.

'Now swear, or I'll shove this up your arse.'

And Lev swore the oath with his hand on a broomstick.

He was assigned not to military duties, but to a work detail. It was revenge for his behaviour, and he accepted it. The journey began on a lorry, and Lev endured hours of sitting on his suitcase. One of the others cut a peephole in the tarpaulin with his penknife and they took turns to look through.

In one place, Ivo, the young Serb, called out that they were in Târgu Jiu, very near the 'Gate of the Kiss', the monument to the fallen soldiers of the First World War. But they didn't stay in the town; the lorry took them up into the mountains, the Southern Sub-Carpathians, where snow still lay a metre deep. Snow-laden pine branches bowed to the ground and paths led off into tree-covered white. He was delivered up to the forest again, but without Imre to watch over him. They were assigned to barracks, which were at least isolated, and again they had to strip to receive their work clothes, this time in front of the others. Ivo got an erection, someone asked in a whisper if he should come and see him in the night, and the men laughed. Lev heard Romanian, Hungarian, Saxon and Banat dialect between the beds. They were given their first shifts, and Lev's was the worst, from midnight to eight in the morning.

It's your own fault. You had to swear on a broom, didn't you? he thought on his first night in the tunnel, as water ran into his rubber boots. He looked at the other men with sympathy: what had these poor devils done to be slaving away here?

A joke about Ceauşescu would suffice.

There were many jokes about the head of state. And yet he'd been the great hope; Romania was the only Warsaw Pact country that hadn't sent troops to Prague and that kept diplomatic relations with the West. But he had obviously lost his mind since visiting China; or else Germany awarding him the Federal Republic's Order of Merit had gone to his head.

They were digging the tunnel for a water main. The water sometimes came up to their knees, and the tools had seen better days. In the morning, a lorry with no tarpaulin cover took them back to the barracks through the icy wind.

What had happened to the fucking tarpaulin, one of the men shouted.

It had still been up the week before, said another.

Lev thought about how often people spoke of darkness in the figurative sense. Only now did he know the true meaning of darkness and cold. This cold that left no desire other than to surrender to it. Back in the barracks, he could hardly move his fingers. When he tried to take off his trousers, they broke in two down the middle. He felt his legs going numb. A pull as if from deep underground. He fell onto the bed and covered his legs, hoping that no one would notice what was happening to him – until the attack passed, and he could move again.

Once you had started to fall you just kept falling, down and down, and if you weren't careful, you would end up like scum that anyone could do with as they pleased. It was time to come back up, and Lev waited for the right moment.

At the start of June, he was given leave again.

His shocked mother held him at arm's length.

'What are they giving you to eat?'

'Enough,' said Lev, trying to reassure her.

'Enough for what work?'

His grandfather, too, eyed him for an unusually long time, and Lev went to look in the mirror. He had grown thinner, wild-eyed. The shorn hair revealed the contours of his skull.

When she told him to disappear, said Bunica, she hadn't meant it literally.

He sat at the table and helped himself to the delicious things made in his honour: paprikash, plaited poppyseed bread, coffee with whipped cream – just like a coffeehouse, said Ferry. Bunica declined cream, saying she wanted to see the colour of the coffee. Lis gasped audibly at the insult. Dorin and his girlfriend had come for the meal. Bredica and her family would not join them until the afternoon. Valea was at the head of the table, where their father used to sit. He asked Lev to tell them about where he was stationed in the mountains (so he put it).

Lev chewed his slice of cake, tried to delay his answer. Valea invested his own military service with a halo of glory. They'd often had to listen to tales of his heroic deeds.

'What do you want me to say?' Lev asked.

How feeble that sounded.

'Well, what you've been doing.'

His brother would know what it meant, being in the tunnel.

'I can't talk about it,' said Lev.

Valea threw him a suspicious glance. And while he went on imagining some kind of struggle for the Socialist Republic, Lev stuffed cake into his mouth.

When they had all gone, and only Ferry and Lev were left at the table, Lis closed all the doors to the main room. As if on cue, his grandfather stubbed out his cigarette and stood up. This was all so strange that even Khalil, curled up on a chair, raised his head. He had spent the mealtime betting on sausage ends and cream, with excellent odds: both Lev and Dorin's girlfriend Silvia had fed him more or less secretly.

'Will you take a little walk with me?' Ferry asked.

Lev, feeling slightly ill from all the food, said, 'Now?'

'Your grandfather needs your help.'

'Yes, of course,' said Lev, pulling himself together.

In the garden, Ferry asked how much leave he had.

'Another week.'

'That should be enough.'

Ferry hunted through a pile of cut branches until he found a suitable walking stick.

Lev waited in silence. Enough for what?

When they had left the garden and the outbuildings, he told him.

'I need someone to take me to a carpark near the Hungarian border.'

The implications struck suddenly.

'You've submitted the papers, though?'

'Papers,' said Ferry scornfully. 'They'll arrive when I'm dead and buried.'

'And what about Lis? What about us?'

'You'll follow on after,' said his grandfather. 'It will be much easier when I'm in the West.'

He didn't ask if that was what they wanted.

Lev thought of the downward spiral. When you fall, you keep on falling. Helping someone flee got you a prison sentence.

'You know I'll drive you anywhere.'

Lis handed him a note with a meaningful look.

'Are you avoiding her, all of a sudden?'

His name in printed letters, a quick sketch of a bird underneath. He would usually have gone to Kato's house on his first day back, maybe even the first hour. Why not this time? His anger, his disappointment at her rejection were gone; they had got lost in the tunnel, like so much else.

At first no one came to the door when he knocked around noon.

The dog gnawed passively at a corn cob, lifting his head only briefly when Lev climbed over the fence rather than trouble the gate. Lev peered in through the broken window pane where the picture of the Eiffel Tower was wedged. Papers were scattered on the kitchen table. A face appeared in the window, watery eyes, bee sting welts all over his neck. Kato's father told him she wasn't at home. Lev wished him well and wondered why they had never got beyond these platitudes. Any attempt to start a conversation beyond question and answer failed. Kato's father gave the impression he had no idea who Lev was or what he was doing here. And worse: he probably had no idea who his daughter really was, either.

Lev started up the dirt path behind the house.

Pale, light green slopes.

A few quick, glass-clear notes.

Only Kato could whistle like that. He whistled back.

Before long, she was standing in front of him. Dismay mingled with joy as she saw how changed he was.

They both started to say the same thing at once: 'I'm sorry…'

'Now we have saved someone from hell,' said Kato.

He was so pleased to see her that at first, he didn't notice. Not until he was back at home, in fact, the encounter echoing inside him. He was calm, and this calmness suppressed everything that was troubling him, the memory of the tunnel, his grandfather's composure and apparent lack of regret as he planned his escape. But beneath this calm lay something unknown, and only in the evening did he become aware that, in her own way, she had been trying to tell him something.

Kato showed him pictures of birds; she must have drawn like a woman possessed in the months he'd been away. Pencil drafts, then more nuanced sketches, and finally watercolour pictures.

Where had she got the paints, he asked.

She seemed surprised, perhaps because he didn't usually say things about her pictures.

From Camil, she said, the paints came from Camil.

Kato leaned back and propped herself on bent arms, leaving him to gather up the pictures strewn across the turf. He put them carefully back in the folder.

'They're really beautiful,' he said, not knowing why that was so hard to say. Drawing these birds must have made her happy.

Now she was silent. Her breath a thin stream of water.

He held her gaze, thinking of the game they had played as children. They called it husband and wife. They kept on playing until one of them said they wanted to stop.

He ran a hand over his forehead, as if he still had hair to brush away.

'Lev, tell me how you are.'

Every morning or evening, depending on the time of his shift, Lev walked in the forest. Leaves were appearing beneath the melting snow. Moss, pine needles. Lev collected pine cones, burrs, stones, kept them under his pillow. Some trees he sought out again and again, like a friend.

The other men warned him not to get lost.

Lev said he knew his way around forests.

Even this one?

All of them.

One day, when he'd been walking for some time, he was stopped in his tracks. There was no other way of describing it; something prevented him from going on. Before him lay a clearing. Two wolves were fighting without a sound. No wind, no birdsong, as if the whole clearing held its breath as it watched along with him – and not just him, everything, the whole expanse of the forest, the weight of the mountain was melting down towards this point.

One wolf radiated calm and strength; it was visibly superior. Before long, the other flattened its ears and began to wag its lowered tail. It bent its back legs, made itself smaller. The victor now stood side-on to it, almost indifferent, its face turned away.

The wolf that had capitulated slunk past him. Strangely, Lev was not afraid. When the birds started singing again, he set off back to the barracks. Should he tell someone? Would it change anything? No, it wouldn't. They lived among wolves. He already knew that.

'Haven't you made any friends?' Kato inquired. She had been listening intently.

There was one man, said Lev, lighting a cigarette. He worked in the kitchen and gave Lev an extra ladle when the food was dished out. And Ivo, a young soldier he was looking after. They were lucky: the tunnel's civil engineer set more store by his humanity than his uniform. He kept trying to make the work easier for them.

Kato took a sheet of paper from the folder and began to draw.

Two wolves in a clearing.

'I think he likes me. Some evenings, we play cards together. He has a light blue motorbike with a sidecar in his garage. But he can't get a driver's licence, his eyesight is too poor.'

'So he needs a licence?' Kato asked.

Lev nodded.

'Come with me tomorrow, to see Milena and Camil.'

It didn't sound like a question.

'Ce să fac? Fac supa de clopot.'

Camil was making his imaginary bell soup. He seemed altered, insofar as Lev, seeing him for only the second time in his life, could judge. His bulk, all that restrained power, stood in stark contrast to the melancholy in his eyes – but the gloom had gone. Nothing about this man was ordinary, and Lev was touched by his deep, hoarse voice.

Kato hugged him, the top of her head level with his shoulders. She had brought her drawings, and Camil, bird watcher and bell cook, examined one after another.

Lev handed Milena a bag of flour.

She cocked her head to one side, smiled.

'What are you doing to get hold of such a thing?'

'Selling his body,' said Kato with exaggerated seriousness.

Both women grinned, and Lev turned away to hide his own laughter. You never went visiting without a gift, but today his offering had an ulterior motive.

Kato and Camil considered the drawings. They were sitting so close their arms touched.

So far, Camil had turned twenty-one blackbird songs into notation with the help of a tuning fork.

Blackbird song in the early morning in the mulberry tree.

Blackbird song in the yard by the well.

Blackbird song by the old mill.

Blackbird song by the stream.

Kato was going to produce a drawing for each melody: the blackbird in the tree, on the well, by the stream, on a gable, in flight, a pair of them in the grass, on a rock. Young, slender blackbirds and older, rounder specimens. The males black with shining beaks and an orange ring around their pupils, giving them a permanent look of slight astonishment. The females brown with flecked underbellies, like a faded sketch.

'Do you lure the birds here?' Lev asked.

'The raisins and sunflower seeds come from my kitchen. They go wild for them, half get scattered, and sparrows and bluetits come along later for the leftovers,' Milena replied. It wasn't a reproach; she was just telling them, for the sake of completeness, where the blackbird food came from.

Camil explained why it was difficult to capture these mierlă melodies. Notes and sounds mingled together, some very quiet, others sharply emphasised. Rolls were a fast repetition of the same note, and trills a rapid sequence of two notes. The stanzas were artfully constructed; sometimes one bird would introduce a new motif, then others would take it up. Most beautiful was the antiphon, a call-and-response duet by two blackbirds. They sang from March to September. So this was their time.

For Camil, the blackbird was a letter from God, pure form, pure tone, devotion. An ephemeral letter, outside the alphabet. If a poet were to master those letters, he would surpass all existing literature.

'You came because you have a question for Camil.'

Kato looked expectantly at Lev.

Without further ado, Lev said he needed a driver's licence.

'Not for himself,' Kato clarified.

'But for…?'

Lev gave a brief outline of his situation. The memory of the tunnel hung like a millstone around his neck. Camil wrote down the name, asked for details, didn't dismiss the idea, didn't say yes or no. Would anything come of all this? Kato seemed to have boundless faith in Camil.

The bar room was filling up. Milena lit candles on the tables. Two men entered the room, and Lev could see from the way Milena's shoulders stiffened that something wasn't right. Kato, talking to Camil, was oblivious. But Camil missed nothing; he slid the radio behind the curtain with his foot.

The men sat down.

The candle on the table guttered.

Milena took their order, walked slowly, deliberately back to the bar, threw her brother a look. And, with a movement that seemed to come from nowhere, he knocked over his glass, its contents spilling across the table and soaking some of the drawings, which sent Kato into a turmoil. Camil fetched a cloth, and meanwhile Milena slipped something under the newspapers on the windowsill. Kato wiped the table, laid the sheets of paper out to dry.

The room had become a stage, where a second, hidden story was playing out behind the obvious action – and now, Camil's left eye was at rest. He chatted to Kato without letting the two men out of his sight. They sat at the table, wordlessly accepting the politeness and the wine they were brought. Milena began to hum a song, the customers laughed, perhaps a little too loudly. Everyone knew who these two were, and Lev, overcome with a sudden fear that they had come for him, took a while to understand. They were interested in Camil, Camil, who was sitting with Kato.

Lev's chair scraped across the floor.

He stood, not knowing what to do.

Kato glanced up in surprise.

Camil looked at him. His eye was not twitching.

The two men got up and left the room.

They hadn't paid.

People had got good at it.

Not seeing, not hearing.

Not thinking.

It was a mark of distinction really, not to think, or hear and see. Because certain others were very good at seeing and hearing; nothing escaped them.

People barely noticed that goods were more expensive, less available. When things happened slowly, you had time to accustom yourself, almost as if nothing was changing, getting worse or scarcer, colder or darker; you grew into it, grew with it.

His grandfather had been waiting six years for his exit visa. Once a month he travelled to Bucharest and joined the queue outside the passport office, each time adopting a new strategy because nothing worked. Recently he had started queuing at three, four in the morning, to be among the first. He had a theory that a dozen or so passports were given out each day, so you had to be among that dozen. He stood through the night outside the passport office, stood for hours in corridors with others who were also hoping, also waiting, with strategies and theories of their own.

Deciding factors might be how many relatives were living abroad, whether you had submitted applications before, been in prison or had a legal case pending, whether you had debts, had enclosed a good letter – or better still, none at all. Also: whether you had bribed the right people, with German currency of course.

Ferry had the impression that, whenever his papers reached the top of the pile, someone shoved them back to the bottom, and so one day he called on the German embassy. The official listened to Ferry's story. Then he stared at him meaningfully, and, making a strange gesture (hands fluttering as if sliding something under the tabletop), said that Romania was a sovereign state, did he understand, a sovereign state, and unfortunately he was not able to help him.

Ferry had considered taking a holiday on the Black Sea coast and fleeing from Bulgaria, where the name of that sea was ‘Chernomorie’, to Turkey. Rumour had it that several different fences had been put up at the green border to confuse would-be defectors. No one could know at what point they had made it to freedom. Ferry decided he was too old to be running around like that.

Did they have everything in the West? Could you really travel anywhere? Was one language enough for a whole country? For all that was sayable and unsayable, obvious and hidden, true and untrue?

Sometimes Mercedes-driving westerners strayed into this area. They looked like they were wearing their clothes for the first time. They admired the landscape, brought coffee, cigarettes and LUX soap to exchange for buffalo cheese, yellow paprika and schnapps; they purchased carpets, woven blankets, traditional embroidered blouses as souvenirs.

What are they talking about, *landscape*? the people in the valley laughed. How could you talk as if it existed outside of you? The landscape had branded itself into Lev’s mind; he carried it with him always. But Ferry said he didn’t care about the land. All he wanted was to get away.

Dear Lord, please let us get the passports. This was one of the prayers most often uttered by the country’s ethnic Germans at that time.

It was time, his mother said on his second to last day at home. Lis moved uncertainly through the room, picking up one thing and then another, until he realised what she wanted him to say.

'Mother, I will be careful.'

'I'm sorry to impose this on you. But…' She paused. 'No one else could be trusted.'

'I know,' said Lev. Dorin wouldn't risk anything now that he was after a bigger flat, and Valea would probably drive Ferry straight to the police station.

'There's one more place on the lorry,' said Lis.

'For you?'

'I'm not going away.'

'Why not?'

'This village is where your father lived. I can't lose him again.'

As Lev wondered whether he felt the same, Khalil slunk into the room. He allowed himself to be stroked, but then ducked away. You always had to look for signs: did an animal love you, or were you were just persuading yourself you belonged together?

'And you?'

'I've got something here, too,' said Lev.

Ferry had no luggage.

'You greet the neighbours, lock up the workshop, wash the dishes, knowing that you're doing it for the last time,' he said.

He liked one particular cup in thin porcelain with a gold rim; it must have come from his mother's tea service. He had dried it with special care, he said, and put it in the cupboard. A cupboard he would never open again.

'Isn't that ridiculous?' Ferry forced a smile. 'A cup telling me what I should have grasped long ago.'

For a long time now, whenever he visited from Sighişoara, he would bring objects for his daughter, things he couldn't bear to part with: his wife's embroidered doilies and pillowcases, a Hapsburg-era dinner service, letters, books.

Lev had looked through the photograph albums with his mother: school photos of Lev, Ferry with his daughter up at the Hohe Rinne, Lev and Ferry under the colonnade in Buziaş, photos of his baptism, his mother's confirmation, his grandfather in uniform… Lev held that page open and asked his mother why part of the collar had been blacked out. She had scribbled over it as a girl, Lis said, ashamed that her father had been in the Waffen SS.

They drove west along nighttime roads. Ferry smoked, the breeze through the window ruffling his hair. Lev tensed whenever headlights appeared in the rear-view mirror. How would someone with a clear conscience drive? He didn't know any more. He was second-guessing every movement.

Imre had taught him to drive a car, they had spent a day driving around valleys and mountains. He had to park and reverse up a gravel track, then Imre gave him a jerry can of petrol, and Lev passed the driving test straight away. Imre had provided the petrol for this journey too, and Lev had the sudden feeling that his friend knew.

At one point, his grandfather asked for a break. Lev turned down a farm track and switched off the engine. Ferry disappeared into the darkness, and Lev did not take his eyes off that darkness until Ferry emerged from it again. The man who got back into the car looked confused, as if he'd lost his way.

'Have you given this proper consideration?' Ferry asked.

Lev nodded, and then, realising that his grandfather couldn't see the nod, translated it into words.

'How long do you still have to serve?'

'A year.'

And did he really want to give away a year of his life.

He wasn't giving it away; he would live out that year one way or another, said Lev. People still had some freedom, even here.

Freedom had to be complete, or it didn't exist, said Ferry.

When around one in the morning they reached the carpark that was their destination, they saw it was closed off.

'What now?' Ferry tried to sound calm and failed.

'We keep going,' Lev decided. 'If the driver is smart, he'll carry on as well. What else is he going to do?'

'Go back. His firm in Germany has already pocketed the money.'

They drove on for ten minutes and reached another carpark.

Now they just had to wait and hope that no police patrol came past.

Without any discussion, Ferry went to hide in the nearby undergrowth. He hesitated by the open car door. Lev had the urge to get out, hug him, stop him from taking this step. But Ferry had already gone.

He wound down the windows. Far-off engine noises, an animal howling, the smell of acacias. Familiar sounds and scents, slightly distorted. They gave him the sense of distance, of somewhere far away. That distant place was within reach. He would never have to go back to the tunnel. Just another car abandoned in a carpark, police searching their house and land, shamefaced ignorance from his brothers, steadfast denial from his mother – and he would be somewhere else, long gone, the memory of the life he had shed dimming, ever more unreal; he could sense how that might feel. Already, this glassy, firmly established world felt dreamlike, and he was filled with the exhilaration of plunging into unknown depths. His stomach knotted into a hard lump. His mind and body drifted in two directions, and it took all his strength to reconnect them.

He threw open the car door just as a lorry pulled into the carpark. How much time had passed?

Not enough.

Lev closed the door with careful nonchalance.

The driver got out, looked searchingly into his face.

When Lev nodded, he asked in German how many were going.

'One,' said Lev, and gave a whistle, the agreed signal.

They wouldn't know for a long time how it had gone. Whether the lorry had made it across the border, whether the stowaways hidden between the load bed and the cabin had held their nerve. Whether the border guards had just checked papers or hauled everything out.

With every kilometre, Lev could feel the distance between him and his grandfather increasing; how final this parting was.

When would they see each other again? Was whatever Ferry hoped to find worth being separated from his family?

The journey back felt long. Lev realised someone was following him. He drove cautiously, not too slow, not too fast. Looked around the interior of Ferry's car: nothing that would give him away. Only himself.

The car overtook and slowed down, forcing him to slow, until it stopped in the middle of a village. A policeman got out.

Fear slammed through Lev's body like a dull blow. He wound the window down, was ordered to step out. Found himself on the road beside the car, not knowing how he'd got there.

He had to show his papers. Where was he going?

'Home.'

How sweet that sounded.

From a friend's house, he'd been to see friends. He was on leave from the military, tomorrow he had to go back, he said, marvelling at his conversational tone.

The policeman, a gaunt man with a moustache, asked where he was serving. When Lev told him, he laughed, gave him a sympathetic clap on the shoulder and let him drive on.

Low clouds. Like a sea you could dive into and away.

Kato was wrapped in an impenetrable silence.

Lev stayed quiet too, as a precaution. Why, when a woman was silent, did he always have the feeling it was something to do with him?

Further downstream, in a spot where the Iza flowed more slowly, they sat down. Kato had brought a jar of honey, and they took turns to spoon some out. When she pulled a picture out of her folder, it took his breath away. For a moment Lev thought she had stolen it from the church, the Virgin Mary looked so real. He admired the translucent skin, the smile, the way the folds of the ice-blue dress fell, looked at Kato's hands, paint under the nails, and wrestled with conflicting feelings. Under Camil's guidance, she had taken a leap forwards. Why couldn't he be pleased for her?

He handed the picture back with the greatest care, putting all his admiration into this gesture.

'When are you coming back?' Kato asked.

He didn't know, he said, thinking that he had to get out of the tunnel before winter came round. They had never spent so long apart as they had that year and, despite everything, it was reassuring to know that she had Milena and Camil. Could Camil get hold of the driver's licence for his boss? A person who tracked down paints for Kato could help him. A person being watched knew the right people.

'When Bunicu died,' said Lev, 'the family sat in the good parlour, neighbours came, friends, acquaintances, half the village, drank schnapps, got up and circled around the body. We children were lifted and passed over him three times. Bunicu was wearing his best suit, his beard was sunken because no one could find his dentures, and every time they circled there seemed to be less of him.'

Eventually he could no longer stand it in the laying-out room. He cried, begged. Bunica pulled off her husband's shoes and socks and made him grasp the dead man's toes. This had to be done, she said, so that death would spare you, so he would know he no longer lived under this roof. Lev could still remember the clammy cold, the blueish nails, shrivelled heels.

'Sometimes I feel as if everything we do is to outwit death. Do you think he understands our signs? Do you think he cares about our circling?'

'Well, we're still here,' said Kato.

'We're here.'

Nesze semmi, fogd meg jól

Four

Lev stepped in every puddle. The larger ones, he jumped in. The water caught wisps of sky, gable ends, electricity masts, the last drops of rain. His shoes were sodden, socks and trouser legs too. In the puddles: a giant on stilts, with a shortened torso and a pin head. On strode Lev, jumping to the rhythm of his anger. Something made him hesitate and he stopped: that puddle might be deep, like the lakes at the saltworks, linked by caves. His grandmother said that water always had its twin brother underground. If he jumped into this one, he would disappear, be gone.

He wanted to be gone. To forget the expression on Fabiu's face.

Fabiu spent his time with lads from the class above, break-times by the kiosk and afternoons outside the station. That didn't have to mean anything. They had been friends, then grew apart; it happened, his mother said. You could be close to someone, and even at a distance you could still be close – but at a distance something had evolved, and he couldn't believe it was enmity.

He had made an effort with Fabiu for weeks, until the effort started to weigh him down. He was trapped in his efforts, which weren't genuine; nothing he said was, every word was uttered for a reason and so felt false. Some days Fabiu was friendly to him, almost like before, but he could see what was going on: they were both trapped in this echo chamber where every sentence missed its mark and rang false.

Lev had gone to the station a few times. Respect was given to the one who was loudest, told the best stories, had done something at the weekend. This never-ending competition of exaggeration and lies struck him as both impressive and repellent. He watched for a while, then stayed away from the group. And soon enough, he found out what happened if you didn't join in.

If you didn't join in, you didn't belong. If you didn't belong, you were an outsider. And outsiders were fair game. There were only two sides: inside and outside, friend and foe. Lev took care to keep his distance at breaktime and was among the first to enter the school building after the gong, taking cover in the crowd. But everyone had to use the toilet sooner or later; as a precaution Lev scarcely drank anything before lunchtime.

The girls had cubicles; the boys peed in a urinal, a long, tiled area that caught the stream and channelled it into a gutter on the floor. Lev had held it in until it hurt, and when the door opened, he wasn't quick enough. They held him up against the wall, his face on the urine-damp tiles. And Fabiu? He let it happen, and then said, 'Enough,' with that cold gaze, that way he had of turning down his face and looking up.

'Stop now, or he'll forget how to walk again.'

On the spur of the moment, Lev took the path to his sister's house. Bredica had birthed her second child that spring. She would have her hands full, wouldn't grill him, and he could dry his wet things in her kitchen.

'Who came off worse, you or the puddles?' she said by way of greeting.

Then they set about their silent tasks, as only siblings could.

Half, his brothers would say. Half siblings.

But with Bredica, he never felt the missing half.

Lev kicked off his shoes, and Bredica handed him socks and put the shoes by the stove. Lev took off his wet trousers, and Bredica gave him a blanket he wrapped around his waist, which would have been embarrassing with anyone else. His sister heated up some soup and toasted bread on the stovetop while he laid the table; her shake of the head telling him that one place was enough. She had already eaten or would eat later, when her husband came home.

The kitchen-living-room housed a divan, a central table, and, to the side, a wood stove also used for cooking. The bed was in the next room, and a loom stood in the hallway, for weaving grey hemp cloth that turned white over the years. Lev's eldest nephew was at nursery and the newborn lay on the sofa, swaddled from the neck down. He looked like one of those wooden dolls with no arms and legs – wrapped up and tied like a bobbin.

After the meal, Bredica washed up. Plates went on the dresser, cutlery was tucked behind a wooden board on the wall. Lev stared at the baby and felt himself grow heavy, as if he were the newborn, arms bound to his sides, legs pressed together, and for a moment he couldn't move, either.

Bredica laid a tangled necklace in front of him, his task ever since she'd discovered he had the patience for it. Perched on the edge of the divan, his sister already had the gestures of older women who laid their hands in their lap, palms up.

While Lev untangled the chain, he told her about their new farm dog, a fiery-red sheepdog Valea had got from a shepherd. The new dog was chained up, barked at everyone, seemed to have it in for Lev in particular. Bredica asked how the dog got on with Khalil, and Lev said the cat gave him a wide berth. The truth was that Lev gave him a wide berth, too; the dog lunged whenever Lev approached the gate. He shot out of the kennel, and Lev felt rather than saw how the chain yanked his neck. Trying to outrun that jerk of the chain, he found himself running from the gate to the front door, and from house to gate.

The shepherd had named him Pax, but no one called him that; he was just 'the new dog'.

Something disturbed the baby, who started to whimper, and Bredica turned and rocked his bandaged body. She still knew how to move without making a sound, a useful skill in her new life. Lighting the fire quietly in the early morning, waking her husband when the coffee was brewed, the semolina porridge made. Countless actions spread over the day: making beds, washing clothes, cooking meals, tending the garden. Some noiselessness had seeped into her core; she had stopped singing, and her smile had become another.

In summer she would sit in the doorway, face to the sun. Back rounded and legs outstretched, hands on the warm wood, face betraying no emotion. Bredica's mother had often sat like this, the neighbours said, in the doorway of the house, which made Lev feel as if he was secretly watching someone sleeping. He didn't care to open the latch on the gate, because it announced his arrival, forcing her to open her eyes. The others did it without a second thought, but he couldn't. She sat in the doorway between two worlds; the one that belonged to her, and the other she belonged to, and over time her face altered, as when darkness leaks in through a gap.

'Talk nicely to him and stay calm as you walk past,' Bredica said in parting.

At first, Lev didn't know what she meant.

'Pax.'

The new dog started barking as Lev approached the gate. He shot out of the kennel, flaming fur, cherry-stone eyes rimmed in yellow. Lev resisted the urge to run to the door, deliberately slowing his pace as he passed the dog – who went on straining and barking.

Lev wandered indecisively around the house, along the loggia into the main room, where social life took place. Stairs led from here to the upper floor (to his brothers' rooms), where he never set foot. He looked briefly into his parents' bedroom, as they still called it, where shutters were closed even during the day, and then went into his own room. He lay on the bed, opened a book. Then he realised it was one of Fabiu's and threw it on the floor. Tiredness overcame him, but he didn't want to sleep; he hadn't taken a nap since the accident. He felt the softness of covers and pillows, unbuttoned his trousers, slid a hand inside. Then he held his hand to his mouth, inhaling his body's new scent, spicy, burning. Every afternoon began this way, with wandering thoughts and half-imagined, repeating fantasies. Scenes playing out in familiar places (with girls he found attractive), sometimes seemed more real than reality. With one difference: he could rewind, improve, repeat, as often as he liked.

Lev sat up.

If a thing was unavoidable, you should get it over with.

His mother was in the summer kitchen, pickling salt cucumbers. Savory, horseradish and dill lay ready, sour-cherry and celery leaves. The jars were drying on tea towels, and two chairs had been moved away from the table as if someone had just been there.

'I'm not going back to school,' he told her.

A fence marked the edge of their land. Lev walked uphill until he could look out over the village. Shingled roofs, yard gates, storks' nests on the electricity masts. The damp grass soaked his trouser legs for the second time that day.

The wind pressed waves into the grass, combed the coat of an animal that stood motionless like Lev's sister in the doorway, on the threshold between inside and outside.

Animals, he thought, always stood on that threshold.

Khalil approached, so casually that he seemed just to be passing through. But then he stopped, his tail an upright question mark against Lev's leg. Lev gave him some of the food he had taken from the kitchen.

His mother had tried arguing, then fallen silent. Her silence was the worst punishment, worse than any telling-off.

Whatever she threatened, he would not go back to school. He was done with it.

If you want to work rather than study, you can go to the forest with your brothers this summer,' she said finally. 'Under one condition.'

'What?'

'Which you will accept.'

He took a deep breath, nodded.

'You finish the school year.'

Everything in him rebelled at the thought.

'After that, we'll see,' said Lis.

There would be no 'after that', Lev was sure of it, and felt triumphant. Could he really be getting away that easily? Soon, there would be no more walk to school, no uniform or morning drills, no more feeling like a dunce when he couldn't get something into his head, no pungent smell of urine in the toilets. He counted up all the 'no mores' and they became a rhyme, a joyful fanfare – until it suddenly occurred to him that he would have to tell Kato.

They met at the Jewish cemetery. Kato had come here often since learning that Jewish families had once made up a quarter of the village.

The disappearing was bad enough.

But the forgetting, she said, was even worse.

The sun had set but the sky was still light, as if it would rise again at any minute and everything would begin anew. The only difference being that soon, he wouldn't have to go to school. 'No more!' his inner voice proclaimed again.

She was so quiet that he took fright. Fright was never good; it didn't speak of a clear conscience. He had to say it now, or he would lose his nerve, but he hesitated, wanting to enjoy her light-heartedness, the strands of hair in the wind, her guileless face turned to him, arms swinging in a rust-red jumper unravelling at the hem.

They forged a path between the graves across damp ground, shoes growing heavy with clinging earth. Kato talked about helping her father shave, and with every word Lev grew more certain that he was betraying her. He had been thinking of himself when he made the decision, not her, not for a second. Then again: he had the right; theirs was a voluntary agreement, not even an agreement, really – it had come about when Kato's father decided that eight years was enough schooling for his daughter. She had been near the top of the class, but from the age of fourteen had to look after the house. Kato bent to his will without complaint. But when convoys of wagons came through the valley, and men and women went from house to house sharpening knives, selling copper pots, mending kettles, then she would spend hours on the swing in the pear tree, and Lev could guess what she was thinking.

Today seemed to have been a good day; they happened, scattered among the procession of dark days. Then a feeling of belonging germinated between her and her father, despite their being strangers trapped together. Kato's father was a beekeeper. Sometimes he would be gone for weeks, at other times he could find no work and drank. Kato feared his rage, triggered by the smallest thing. She spent all the time she could at Lev's house, where Lis taught her to cook, bake, preserve – everything you needed to run a household.

Who would help her to learn now? Twice a week, Lev went through schoolwork with her. He read out his notes and she asked questions. Her questions helped him understand the material, and his marks improved. Anger boiled up in him. After all, it wasn't his fault that her father couldn't see how clever she was. Lev looked at the raw skin on her hands, nails cut (or bitten?) much too short, and all at once the exuberant strands of hair flattened, as did the light in her eyes. Kato knew what was coming; her body had already absorbed this knowledge. Maybe he didn't have to say anything, maybe he could get out of having to explain. When he stopped and turned to look at her, the joy had vanished from her face.

At the start of the summer holidays, he waited on the station platform with his brothers, Dorin and Valea. A dozen other men camped there with bags and rucksacks. The woman at the station kiosk was wearing her dressing gown, curlers in her hair as she sold cigarettes, matches, beer.

They boarded the train, and Lev followed his brothers to a four-seater. The benches were wooden, windows open. Bottles of schnapps circulated, and someone played a jaw harp. Lev stretched his back, trying to look as if he'd done the journey many times. The train began to move, the station grew legs, the church steeple appeared and was gone at once. Just before the viaduct, Lev heard a whistle, glass-clear, piercing; leaping up, he saw her beside the track. Kato waved to him, and he forgot his pretend reserve and waved wildly back, not caring about the ridicule in his brothers' eyes. The green trees blurred into a ribbon, mingling with strips of cornflowers. Everything was movement and anticipation.

Around thirty men changed onto the Mocănița line. The valley widened and the forest train crawled along it, the regular jolts making Lev drowsy. Every so often the greenish white river changed sides. The journey stopped only to quench the locomotive's thirst.

At their destination, Lev lost sight of his brothers. Dorin reappeared outside a chapel. The wooden huts were twilit and cold inside. Lev went to put his rucksack on the camp bed next to his brother's, but someone got there first. Jostled, he was about to move on when he heard Dorin's voice.

'Get lost, can't you see my brother's sleeping here?'

The man took his bag and kept walking.

Lev wanted to thank Dorin, but Dorin didn't look up.

The sun cut a bright triangle into the clearing where they assembled. The surrounding noise rose and swelled without growing louder, like applause from a distant theatre or marbles poured onto soft ground. Some smoked, others chatted, and then everyone began to move. After twenty minutes or so they reached the work site. A man with red-blond hair and long boots divided them into groups and explained the safety procedures. Then Lev was given an axe with a thick, greasy handle, and the job of chopping smaller branches off felled spruce trunks. That became his movement for the rest of the day. Raising his arms, seeing a piece of sky, striking, tucking the hair behind his ear, carrying the branches to the collection site. Pausing – not too long, not long enough for someone to think the work too hard for him – then slowly, a little slower than necessary, returning to the felled trunk, amid the howl of chainsaws, the chopping and sawing. Now and again, someone let out a loud cry and a tree fell to the forest floor.

Some of the men sat together in the break, while others kept their distance. Lev had no desire for company. He had brought bread, cheese and boiled eggs from his provisions, sat on a log, closed his eyes.

Marbles clacking, distant voices. Birds.

Their song was a sonar, sounding the depths of the forest.

He was hungry but barely ate. He thought of his father, tried to imagine him felling trees, wondered which hut he had slept in, which men had been his friends, and hoped that he'd inherited something of his father's strength and ability. Lev buried his head in his hands, tried to swallow the sobs rising in his throat. Everything hurt, and he had no idea how he was going to get through the rest of the day.

The man who gave the orders was called Imre. In the forest, his word was law. He didn't have to assert his authority through volume or strength; it was simply there.

'You there,' he called out, and instinct told Lev that he was being addressed. He lowered the axe, with which he had just hacked unsuccessfully at a stubborn branch.

'Who are you?'

Lev stretched his back, said his full name.

No worker looked up, but they were clearly listening, every one of them.

Imre told Lev to come with him and Lev followed, trying to shake off the humiliation. Now he would be sent home, on the very first day, and in his mind's eye he saw the new dog lunging, his mother greeting him, gratified because she'd known he wouldn't last.

As they walked to a wooden hut, Lev studied the man's back, his broad shoulders, powerful arms, wide gait. It was a forest way of walking: he stalked. This man on tarmac? Unimaginable.

Inside, the hut was surprisingly bright. Books and papers lay on a desk, and another round table stood in the corner. There was a place for cooking, too, a sideboard with crockery. When Imre turned round, Lev saw something that might have been a smile, or perhaps doubt. He hoped this man couldn't see how tired he was, how dispirited.

'Listen, boy, I don't know why you're here, but one thing I do know: I have no desire to send you back to your mother missing a leg. In the afternoons, you're going to help me.'

'With what?'

Imre turned to the pile of papers on the desk.

'This, for a start.'

That evening, Lev went for a walk.

The trees were dark, looming figures. The noises of the forest overlaid the men's conversations, the rustling leaves, the branches that kept moving even when all was still.

Felled trees lay beside and on top of one another. The scene was a desolate one, needles and branches strewn everywhere. One tree had toppled, uprooting itself, and on the ground something gleamed, a piece of metal reflecting the evening sky. The earth was damp around the ripped stubs, roots sticking into the air. It came to him that it was wrong to fell a tree. He laid a hand on the trunk, on the bark; something in this tree was alive, would live on forever, long after it had been processed.

Lev walked uphill but didn't arrive. There was no arrival here, no place where you could look out over hills and villages. He decided to stop, before he lost his way and the loggers had to come looking for him and made him the butt of their jokes. He sat on a root, ate the apple he had brought. If Khalil was here, he would have jumped onto his lap and curled up. When Lev stayed still, the cat would tip his head back, revealing deep, white neck fur. Lev never tired of studying the markings in his fur, shorter around the nose with a neat depression in the cartilage as if left by a fingernail.

Could you say farewell to animals?

Not to a cat.

Tonight, Khalil would find his bed empty. He would come back tomorrow, and the next day, not knowing where Lev had gone.

The railwaymen communicated through whistles. The wagons had been loaded with trunks, spruce and fir. The train driver leaned out of the window, his eyes streaming. He had to keep scanning the tracks for fallen rocks and trees. Going down into the valley, the braking distance was long.

A wail; steam issued from the locomotive, the train moved off, and, without Lev consciously deciding, his legs started to move: he ran beside the track until he was out of breath and the train out of sight. Was this feeling homesickness, or just something like it?

The days started early and the nights were wearisome. Someone was always snoring, someone always going out to relieve himself, two people always talking across their beds.

'That's how it is,' his brothers said. You got used to it.

In the mornings, Lev hacked off branches until it felt as if the branches had hacked off his arms, for all the use they were by lunchtime. In the afternoons, Imre fetched him. Lev waited impatiently for this moment, hiding that emotion from the others, though not himself. Imre quickly worked out how Lev could be of use. State regulations reached every place, even the forest, and not a week went by without official post. Imre threw it all in a cardboard box, hoping it wasn't important. Lev sorted through the papers, put those requiring action in front of Imre, and worked out a system for the ones that simply accumulated legal clauses or annulled previous regulations. Coffee breaks passed in silence. It was only when they walked through the forest that Imre lost his taciturnity.

Had Lev ever wondered, he said, why you knock on wood to swear to something, or ward something off – and did he know why judges bang a hammer on a block of wood? No? To this day, courts derived their power from the trunks they were felling here. People knew, or at any rate had an inkling, that their own fate depended on the trees.

Lev learned that you could read mild, dry, frosty or wet years from the rings, which showed when a tree had grown hesitantly or shot up. Imre smoked as he talked, the smoke escaping with the words. The pale part, the sapwood, was young, active wood. With age, the tissue lost its life force and in some species was transformed into heartwood. This dark, inner part of a trunk was dead, but the dead wood carried the living.

Trees, said Imre, were dying even as they grew.

A trembling heralded the fall. A crack like pulling a tooth. A rustling roar. Silence.

It took Lev a while to understand these processes. In the early days he stood around cluelessly while all the others knew what they were doing. The men felled a tree with precisely coordinated movements, stripped the bark, rounded the edges so the trunks could slide downhill to the collecting point. When tools were handed out, the others knew what they needed in advance, stripping iron, splitting wedge, cant hook, chainsaw. The worst thing was to stand there pretending he knew what was what, while knowing nothing at all, just waiting for someone to explain, hopefully without being too obvious about it.

Time and again, one of the men would help him out. A logger called Georg told the best stories – kasska, he called them – and he demonstrated the crucial thing about removing branches: to check if they were intertwined, taut, because a branch could spring loose with great force. Someone from the Republic of Moldova, whose name was impossible to remember, began to help him, and the breaks between trees grew longer. Those breaks were spent tool in hand, so it looked like you were working.

Dorin shared out their provisions, warmed up the tins of food they had brought, cooked polenta. His brother Valea treated Lev just as he did at home: like he didn't exist.

Lev settled into this rhythm, and nothing was more beautiful than a day when everything fell into place, and he too barely needed to speak.

One day, he was given the job of sweeping the huts.

After a while, the flow of his movements splintered and he paused. Stripes of sunlight moved slowly across the floor, so little light for a room full of beds. Bending felt difficult. Socks and magazines lay under the camp beds, a bottle rolled away across the room as he tried to pick it up. The floor must be on a slant, thought Lev – then a cramp in his middle rooted him to the spot. The broom fell.

'What's up?' asked the man from Moldova.

'Nothing.'

The man's face drifted apart.

Lev pressed his hands to his belly. He started to feel sick.

'When was the last time you went to the toilet?'

Lev turned red, didn't reply.

The Moldovan fetched something, took him by the arm and led him like a donkey on a rope to the pit latrine.

'Here,' he said, pressing strips of newspaper into his hand. 'You go and squat in there and, to put it politely, empty your bowels.'

Hanging his head, Lev felt his guts rumbling. He hadn't been for a week. At first he'd forgotten, and then it had become embarrassing, because he saw how the men went to the little shacks, sometimes in twos or threes. The instant the Moldovan left he pulled down his trousers and crouched over the ditch, grateful that no one came and he remained alone.

Lev lay awake, waiting for the morning. He kept his clothes on at night; they all did here. Outside the window, the sounds of light were gathering. A mouse ran across the bed, fast, noiseless, before he had time to react.

He pulled the cover over his head and tried to imagine Kato's face, but couldn't at will. In the forest, the things that were his retreated; he was no more than a few hours from home, but this clearing felt like the furthest flung place in the world. He thought of Kato's pale grey eyes, her bitten fingernails, the protruding bones of her wrist.

They used to play a game they called husband and wife. They went to the Iza, a spot far from the village where the water pooled. They floated, tried to dunk each other, Lev pretended he didn't have the strength, then sought revenge – but she was long gone to the middle of the river and then on the other side, below the dark, wooded slope. Sand collected on that bank, and he would find her motionless in the silt like a lizard. He lay beside her, sand moulding to his back. Bravado overcame him, he was awake, wide awake, river sounds, forest sounds, her breathing, and in one quick movement he rolled onto her. The three moles on her cheek continued all the way to her belly, he traced the line with his hand. She kept her eyes shut, and he stayed silent too, pressing his lower body against her, until she turned the game around. Now she was on top of him, pressing herself onto him, and he felt her weight as she had felt his. From the meadows came the sound of a million crickets, a buzzing that went through his whole body.

Lev put his shoes on quietly and went out.

At this hour, the birds took flight, and paths began to be distinguishable from their surroundings. A stream ran behind the boulders. There was no sound but the water; Lev gave a start when Imre suddenly appeared at his side. Without a word of greeting, they went to the bank. Lev wetted only face, neck and hands, while Imre washed his upper body, then handed him the towel, signalling that Lev should go with him. In the hut, he put a pot of coffee on the stove. They waited in silence for the water to boil and the grounds to settle.

The morning was a great Before: before the others woke and prepared food for the day, before the chainsaws started up, the blows of the axe, before the lunch break when Imre would fetch him, before it grew dark and he again lay in the hut with the others, memories of home crowding in.

He wondered what it would be like to stay forever in the forest.

'Why are you really here?' Imre asked.

Dorin had told him Imre's story.

Did Lev imagine that someone like Imre would voluntarily spend his life here, cut off from the world?

'Does he seem like a happy person to you?' Dorin asked.

Lev had never thought about it. Could you divide people into happy and unhappy? How would you tell? Imre was taciturn, kept to himself. But as far as Lev could see, so did Bredica, Dorin, Valea, Bunica, Ferry and his mother Lis. Everyone. They didn't share the essential things. He and Kato were no different, though he sometimes wished they were.

Imre was the first to rise and the last to go to bed. The light in his hut often burned late into the night. Though this man hardly seemed to sleep, he wasn't above any kind of work. More than once, Lev had watched with bated breath as he put himself in situations anyone else would have avoided.

Imre had a son, said Dorin, who'd lost his life at eight years old.

'How?' Lev asked.

'A car accident.'

His brother paused.

'Imre was driving.'

Cries, a scrabble of feet, something like playground noise. The face of the man sitting opposite changed. Imre, who had been studying a chart, swore and ran outside.

The loggers had formed a circle. Lev crouched and looked between their legs. It was no surprise that Valea had got into a brawl, just that he'd been defeated. Imre pulled the fighters apart and ordered the onlookers to stop standing uselessly in the way. Lábatlankodni, he shouted, which the man beside Lev translated as 'you are as if legless'. The men dispersed reluctantly, as if hoping the brawl might flare up again.

'You two just can't let it be, can you?' said Imre, helping Valea up.

Valea didn't fend him off, but also did nothing to help, so it took all Imre's strength to support him. He told Lev to get some hot water and a cloth.

After treating the wound above Valea's eye and cleaning his face, Imre poured him a shot of schnapps.

'Listen, I need to punish both of you. You'll be mending tools – otherwise I'll have a punch-up on my hands here every day.'

Valea just shrugged and put his feet up on a chair. Even now, even here, he showed no weakness. Sometimes Lev feared that his father had been like that, unapproachable, hostile, and that he'd just forgotten how he was.

'What was the problem?' Imre asked.

'Nothing, he's just a son of a bitch.'

'You all are.'

The two men laughed.

Valea, who thus far had taken no notice of Lev, now turned and told him to get lost. Lev obeyed reluctantly. The men waiting outside the hut watched him walk away. Lev guessed what they were thinking: he wasn't just Valea and Dorin's brother, he was the boy who had made it inside Imre's hut in no time at all.

Although his brothers were among the youngest loggers, they got the best tools, and when wine was brought out in the evening, theirs were the first glasses to be filled. When a young worker, like Lev there for the first time, tried to sit with them, someone pointed out who Lev and his brothers were. You could tell from the lavishly decorated gates of their houses that his family was not just any family. Bunica left no one in any doubt about this: as far back as the eighteenth century, her ancestors had worked with Austrian and Zipser German colonists, planting trees, thinning out woodland, shipping trunks on rafts along the Tisza – from the Carpathian forests to Novi Sad.

Lev understood that here, this story carried some weight. That here, too, it was a story – but one that was believed.

Every Friday felled wood was transported out, food deliveries arrived, workers left for home. Every Friday Lev stood by the train, feeling that tug below his navel calling him away. A few men stayed in the logging area at the weekend, because it was too far to go, or nothing was waiting for them, or, like his brothers, because they wanted to earn overtime. If Lev went to Imre's hut, Imre was usually absorbed in a book and sent him away. He learned how to play cards – whist and poker – and finally slept through the night. In the evenings, Georg told his stories. Of water sprites and soul-birds, of fog witches who turned people into stone.

Lev liked the reduced troop: everything was quieter, more well-practised, and at lunchtime he didn't withdraw, but ate his bread with the others. He came to trust Matthis in particular, the worker who had tried to sit beside his brothers. They talked as if they'd known each other a long time. Nobody here used boasting as a way to intimidate; the way the lads at school showed off seemed ridiculous. They bragged about their weekends but had probably done nothing more than lie in bed, indulging in some fantasy or other. He had been reluctant to acknowledge that Fabiu hadn't been his friend for a long time; their bonds had been forged in childhood and, if he was honest, he no longer liked the person Fabiu had become.

One Sunday morning he woke early and roused Matthis. They slipped out of the hut and walked through the forest. Lev knew how to get his bearings now, found the path without needing breadcrumbs or pebbles. Matthis was two years older and had finished school already. His forebears came from Slovakia, had been miners and woodsmen, but he wanted to study in Sibiu and become a teacher, so that the school in Viseu de Sus could still offer lessons in German. Lev could see he was excited, but also afraid. They made a list of things you didn't need to be afraid of (a forest at night, fog witches, moving to a new city), and resolved not to build their lives around fear.

After three quarters of an hour, they reached the lookout point. They sat on a rock and watched the sun rise over the mountains. Two ravens performed a sky dance, never more than two wingspans apart, hovering, plunging, climbing, circling one another and then falling like black stones.

Entering a forest was like stepping into a church. Your sense of time was lost, affiliations suspended. The forest was inside, everything else outside. Just a few weeks ago, Lev would have claimed it was the other way around. His house and yard, the village, his family, Kato – they existed somewhere on the other side of this forest, in an unreal, almost meaningless world.

Some trees were more forbidding than any person he knew. Others leaned together, or grew in a particular direction out of deference, care or need, developing qualities that set them apart from the others. Lev was learning to see the trees as individuals, not just a mass of forest.

Imre pointed out mosses, fungi, beetles and insects, flowers such as violets or wood anemones. If a tree was two hundred years old, leaves had fallen and new leaves unfurled two hundred times; this source of nourishment had been withstanding winds, enduring long winters, storms, droughts and rains harder and more relentless than humans could imagine. When a tree died, it became a home to animals.

Imre was different. Had a different language, a different way of looking at things. You saw it in the books in his hut, the crockery he used. In one of their coffee breaks, Lev had asked why he was here. For a while, Imre looked as if he wouldn't answer, and Lev was sorry he'd broken their silence.

He was searching for an underground river, said Imre. One that you drank from to forget your past.

Every evening Lev roamed through the forest, until he came across a tree that seemed to be waiting for him. He leaned against the trunk, looked up at the branches, the crown, hoping it would not meet the same fate as those waiting lower down the hill, stripped of bark and branches, to be carried away on the narrow-gauge railway. And if that did happen, the wood would remember the whirring song of the wood warbler, which you rarely saw, but always heard, the knocking of the black woodpecker with its deep red crown, the fearless, inquisitive call of the greenfinches in the spinneys by the river. Sometimes he felt the tree was answering him. Without knowing how this had come about, he had gone over to the other side of nature.

The scream went through Lev like a sharp blade. He gave his legs the order to run. One step, then another. Don't stand still, don't turn around, keep going.

Matthis was lying on the ground. Imre knelt beside him, was still examining him as men arrived with a stretcher. They picked up the injured boy and carried him to a van, which would take him to the nearest hospital. Matthis was unconscious, he'd been struck on the head by a falling branch.

No one did any more work that day. They sat around, smoking, talking. One man said: the devil was in that wood. When Imre returned, he set bottles of schnapps down on the table, and it was clear they weren't going to bed until the bottles were empty.

'He's in a coma. If he's lucky, he'll wake up and be able to walk, talk, and if not…'

'I didn't see him,' said one of the men. 'I…'

'It was a deadwood branch,' Imre interrupted.

'But what if…?'

'Everyone will confirm it was an accident.'

Those standing around agreed, but Imre's words didn't reach the man who had felled the tree and not seen Matthis. Lev knew this sense of guilt that nothing could take away. Valea slid a full glass of schnapps over. When Lev had drained it, his brother threw him a glance he couldn't read and refilled the glass.

Lev tipped it down in one and began to hiccup.

The scent of lavender, the sound of water rushing into a tub; Matthis' face, his motionless body changing into another body, another face.

He hadn't thought of her in a long time.

Night. Dark, unstable night. Something was spinning, his stomach, his head, the bed, the hut, the earth. Lev stretched a leg out of the bed and the spinning slowed. Lonja and Silas suddenly appeared. They had been hidden away in this turning of things, in a corner of his consciousness, and it had taken a deliberate halt, a slowing of the world for them to reemerge.

He jerked upright, shuffled into his shoes, thought, I am shuffling into my shoes, felt his way past beds that stood close together, closer than usual, banged his knee, heard swearing, swore back, opened the door and stumbled out into the forest. Why *into* the forest, he thought, you're in it already, you're always in the forest, and this thought seemed so ridiculous that he almost laughed. He tripped over something, fell, scrambled up and walked on until he reached the chapel. Through the side window, he looked for the portrait above the altar. She was there, hanging somewhere in this darkness, Empress Elisabeth. Lev sank to his knees and threw up.

Imre found him in the morning. Walked him to his hut, handed him a blanket.

They didn't speak, and Lev was glad, because everything hurt and the night had chilled his whole body, especially his bare feet. He leaned back in his chair and drank the coffee Imre had made, the most delicious he'd ever tasted.

'Listen, lad, I'm going to give you some advice. Take the next train. You need to get away from here while you can. Eventually you won't be able to. The forest will keep you for itself, you'll go on dreaming of another life, but there'll be no path out.'

Loggers gathered on the platform as they did every Friday. Dirty, unkempt and yet bound to one another, a single sworn community. The train had been waiting for some time. The driver shunted, eyes streaming; additional wagons were coupled. When the locomotive blew its whistle, Lev flinched. He had washed in the stream, bidden farewell to everything, the woodpile, his favourite trees, Imre's hut. He took in the sounds once more, the silence that wasn't silence; birds, the marble sound the leaves made, wind in the pines.

Word had reached them that Matthis was awake. Imre had made out a cheque, and Lev wrote the card to go with it. He might not heal in time for the start of the semester in Sibiu, but he was alive, awake, talking, and Lev, who since Matthis's accident had been eyeing every tree with suspicion, was overjoyed.

He made a list of categories for the incoming post, and explained the filing system to Imre. So he could manage on his own, just in case.

Yes, just in case, Imre repeated.

He felt the banknotes in his trouser pocket, the summer's wages. Dorin was staying until the end of the month; Valea was going home for the weekend. And Lev?

'See you next week,' said Lev.

'See you next week,' Imre repeated.

How easy it was to say something that wasn't true.

Lev walked slowly towards Kato, rather slower than befitted his joy. Was he surprised to see her? Was he embarrassed at her hugging him on the platform in front of the other men? He returned the hug, returned her gaze, or perhaps it was the other way round: she returned his hug, his gaze. It was impossible to tell.

'How did you know…?'

'I've been waiting every Friday.'

'All summer?'

She nodded.

Someone was jostling him, as amicable as a greeting, and he didn't have to look up to know who it was. All at once his shyness was gone; he had seen and done so much, and it would take a long time for him to tell Kato everything (really, everything?).

'Are you going back?'

No, said Lev and thought her tread lightened at the news. Something new was combining inside him, too, a security, the anticipation of home. The lanes were dry and dusty, the meadows mown, the hay long since brought in. And at home, something was different too: no barking.

'Pax was set free for the summer,' said Kato.

He wasn't exactly keen to encounter the dog without its chain, but sensed that this had been a time of independence for his mother, who had been free to make her own decisions. It stung, mind, to see how effortlessly everything had gone on without him.

Lis came out from the loggia, took his rucksack. He didn't have to tell her if he was staying, if he was going back to school; she could see it in him. He would grasp the magnitude of her relief only later.

Bunica said he smelled terrible. All the same, she took him in her arms, and surprised at this unaccustomed tenderness from his grandmother, he didn't see right away what was happening in the yard. His mother's face darkened; Kato's hands balled into fists.

Valea had put the dog back on the chain.

Pax barked, resisted, head and body each going its own way, strangely, like two parts that didn't fit together. He snapped at Valea, who gave the dog a kick.

The next morning, Lev woke early, amazed to find the concert of birds absent. He could hear a gentle breeze.

Force four, thought Lev, moves small branches.

He lay in bed, in the quiet house, the clean room, feeling both quiet and cleanliness as physical sensations. No one was up, and floorboards creaked as the house performed its usual morning stretches.

Lev walked barefoot down the corridor to the main room. Yesterday evening, Lis's things had been scattered across the table, magazines, knitting needles, notebooks; now everything was gone. Khalil was asleep on a chair cushion.

The previous evening the cat had also appeared the instant Lev walked in, and when he unpacked his rucksack, Khalil sniffed his dirty clothes and then peed on them without hesitation. He made his feelings very clear. Lev's mother didn't find it funny. The cat had barely shown his face over the last few weeks, she said, and now he waltzed back in with these bad manners.

A figure was approaching the kennel. The outlines of hen house, shed and gate were hazy in the morning mist – and for a moment standing at the window he thought he was dreaming, because no sound came from the kennel.

Pax trotted out, waited patiently for the chain to be removed.

The figure went into the back garden, stopped and patted its leg encouragingly. The dog wavered, as if unable to shake off the weight of the chain so quickly. He pricked up his ears, let out a little whimper. Then he followed.

Lev hastily pulled the curtain aside.

Kato looked up at the window, pressing a warning finger to her lips.

Da kamen alle Vögel und wilden Tiere herbei, und die Katze wählte jetzt die schönsten, farbigsten Federn und machte daraus einen Mantel, der glitzerte und glänzte wie der Sternenhimmel, und gab ihn dem Jungen.

Three

Lev had to rest.

It sounded so simple.

Rest at night. Rest in the day. Rest.

A bed with an adjustable back was set up. He needed to be quiet, away from everything and everyone, like a stowaway hiding on a ship.

Was he being hidden?

When his mother entered the room, she put on a smile at the threshold. A smile that was meant to reassure, a smile like two hands cupped above her eyes, warm, dark. His brothers seldom came, and when they did, said little. Not that they had said much in all the years before, years in which he'd walked, sat, run, swum in the river with the others – those boys who paid visits, then came less often, then not at all. Why should they? There was nothing new here. He had nothing to tell, and to be honest, he didn't want to hear their stories. The time before seemed like a trial period. At some point he must have fallen out of line, and now he was surplus to requirements, stored in a back room. Maybe one day, even his mother would forget. Her visits would grow less frequent and then stop. Eventually he would be found, someone would push open the door and say hang on, there's someone in here. The others would come to look and say, Lev, it's Lev, we forgot about Lev.

His room had a window, but from the bed he could only see the corrugated iron of the shed, sometimes pigeons, light swelling in the morning and waning later. Lev thought about what it had been like to get out of bed without giving his legs a second thought as they carried him to the bathroom, the kitchen; what it was like to walk downstairs, jump down the steps from the loggia day after day, to head across the yard and through the gate onto the street. To roam in the mountains with friends after school, the way the hills rose up alongside, ahead and behind, always in motion, just as they were. His body in space, somewhere between these turning, tumbling, swaying hills.

He remembered them spraying each other with water from streams until their clothes clung to their bodies. Searching shepherds' huts, flattening anthills, stealing eggs from birds' nests. And he remembered tying cockchafers to a pencil with a length of thread and watching them fly in circles. It's a fan, they shouted, holding the cockchafers in front of each other's faces. How long it took for the creatures to wear themselves out. When they finally hung from the pencil, the boys dropped them along with the thread. They had bound the cockchafers' legs, thought Lev. Now someone large had bound his legs, to show him how it felt. And Lev turned to the wall and hid his face.

He woke at six, to the sound of his mother's tread (quiet, hurried footsteps) in the hallway. Lightbulbs hummed, water boiled, bedclothes were shaken out and hung in the window. The wind brushed the loggia's pillars and plants, slammed doors. Then came his brothers' feet on the stairs, and finally his sister's. Cocks crowing, hooves out on the street. Someone might call up to an open window, or people chatted – words walking away from one another and words approaching. The dog lunged, the taut chain clanged, the yard gate opened. The postman's voice, his mother's laughter. Lev saw her in his mind's eye, walking up the steps to the house, opening the post as she went, putting it on the table in the main room. The smell of toast would float through the house, and of polenta cooked until firm enough to slice with a thread. His brothers asking for cream, and when they had finished, his mother and Bredica washing up. Finally, when everyone had gone, the two women would eat some of the preserved quinces. There followed a long silence. Lev could only hear his own breathing, the rustle of bedclothes when he moved, sometimes birds or a distant knocking. He lengthened his limbs until he became longer than the bed, than the house, until he didn't fit inside at all. Someone had jammed him into this dolls' house, Lev the giant, Lev, conqueror of the world.

Then the rhythm of the house started up again, the sounds telling him what was happening indoors, who had come to visit, who was arguing with whom, was silent or had long since left. So it went on until evening. Lev had no idea how he was supposed to fall asleep, having lain in bed all day. His mother read to him, they prayed together, and then she gave him a goodnight kiss on the forehead. His door stayed open a crack, and light entered the room when his sister had to go to the toilet, or his mother did some final bit of housework, or when Valea went out late. At first Lev matched the sounds to actions, but soon they translated themselves into images, so quickly that he didn't need to think. Now and then, a sound he didn't recognise mingled with the breathing of the house. Some nights he had the impression that an animal was slinking down the hallway, and listened, startled, but when he couldn't hear anything, decided that he must have imagined it. Lev recognised that the house was awake at night, too. That they were both awake and listening.

His mother washed him, shook up the pillows, changed the sheets. Brought food, water, the chamber pot, fresh pyjamas, books. Each time she came in, she stroked his face, and he inhaled kitchen smells, garden smells, street smells. The dry, cold days of late autumn turned to winter, and Lev thought he heard snow falling outside his closed window. Snow silenced noises close by, brought those further away much closer. Frost came, every step a bright crunch, and the hard, scraping blows of the snow shovel cut through the mornings.

His sister scattered sunflower seeds outside Lev's window, inviting sparrows and bluetits. They announced their arrival with calls, perhaps telling each other that there was food here, perhaps bringing a message for Lev. They came in turn, first bluetits, then sparrows, one bird after another calling, pecking, taking flight, and for the duration of this show, Lev was with them on the other side of the window, on the other side of the room.

Had she gone mad? Valea scolded her for feeding sunflower seeds to birds, was she going to put the cheese out on the windowsill next, the bread, the milk? The birds kept on coming to the window for a few days more, they pecked at the glass. Did Lev not understand they were hungry? He put his hands over his ears and closed his eyes until the window stayed empty.

He remembered one birthday he had spent at the Iza with his siblings. They looked for stones along the riverbank, and when Valea found an especially beautiful one and showed it to him, Lev took it from his hand, admired it, and then quickly swung his arm back and hurled it into the water. He regretted it when he saw Valea's tears, and he regretted it now, convinced that they could have been friends, were it not for that.

At this time of year, the adults didn't sit on the bench outside the gate. Evening life played out in the main room. Lev heard their voices. Occasionally someone would play the accordion, and the scent of cigarette smoke floated through the rooms. Some guests came to see him, but for short visits; he was to be viewed, like a piece of furniture.

Lev couldn't sleep, laced his fingers behind his head, stared at the ceiling, listened to the breathing of the house. He didn't know if he was sleeping, dreaming or awake, whether he even was. Those were the good nights. Nights when everything dissolved: thoughts, body, bed, room, house. He dissolved, mingling with the darkness, the night, and something beyond the night.

Recently, he had started hearing footsteps in the main room early in the morning. Quiet steps, the rustle of a dressing gown, the front door. A few minutes later, the sounds were repeated in reverse: front door, rustle, footsteps. The garden privy wasn't generally used at night, so whoever needed to go wanted to be alone. Was it his sister? No one else in the family could open the door so quietly (the handle needed a gentle lift). Some people didn't care how much noise they made. His brothers were loud in everything, treading heavily, banging glasses down on the table, shouting at each other through closed doors. Not his sister. Things inclined towards her, plates gave themselves into her hands, the floor slid itself under her feet, and when she had something to say, she would walk the necessary steps to meet the other person.

'Bredica?'

The footsteps paused outside the door.

'Bredica?'

She was at his bedside in an instant, as if the space between door and bed didn't exist. He felt her sit down before he could make out her face in the dark.

'How did you know it was me?'

'I have night eyes.'

She stifled a laugh.

'Are you ill?' asked Lev.

'Worse.'

What could be worse? he wondered.

She shook her head, stroked his face. He turned away. Why did everyone stroke him – why didn't they talk to him?

'Whatever it is, you have to tell Mother.'

But Bredica said nothing. Two more weeks of nocturnal garden visits went by before she finally spoke.

It began with the sound of feet, the lighting of the fire, water boiling, tea brewing, the clink of spoons, sugar, names being called out, tiredness. It began with bowls, cloths, cups, knives. Hands grasped shovels, brooms, kettles, swept ashes and snow, loosened earth. They scattered maize kernels for the chickens, hay for the cows, darned cloths, mopped floors, washed crockery, knocked in nails, cracked nuts, carried wood, piled corncobs, peeled potatoes, raised glasses to mouths.

Lev inventoried the noises. He knew their sequence, their purposes. His mother, always busy, barely made any noise. Dorin was boisterous; you always knew when he was there – and Valea was a shadow darkening the house. Bredica was the melody, the only one who found things to laugh at, who sang a song or told a story. Sometimes she sat on his bed in the middle of the day. Most people brought a limited supply of time, measured and packed up in advance. He could tell from the moment they appeared in the doorway how long they would stay. It was written on the visitor's face, in their legs, hands, back. He saw it in their glances at the window, in the position of their feet, half turned to the door. They popped in, they dropped by, they were passing, just quickly, for a moment. Bredica had no time limit. She brought him necklaces and bracelets that had tied themselves in knots in her jewellery box, as if through some miraculous will of their own, and patiently he untangled them. She sat, he budged over, they chatted.

The woman next door slept with her calf in the room.

Nelu's belly is rounder than the cheeses he makes.

Aunty Anuța swears her picture of the Virgin Mary is weeping.

The cooper has died.

Sigi hardly has a tooth left in his head.

The Iza has frozen over.

The ghost appeared in Grandmother's room again.

When Bredica told stories, they grew like vines into Lev's room, reaching all the way to his bed. Until night and silence once more laid themselves over the house and another morning came. Until the light arrived with tentative words, the boiling of water, a little sugar, a little warmth. And it all began again.

His sister's wedding was set for the middle of December, a winter wedding, an ice wedding, she called it.

Bunica came to let out her granddaughter's skirt, because if you looked closely, you could see Bredica's belly, a dome on which she laid her hands from time to time. Lev didn't see the neighbour women coming to discuss the wedding meal with his mother, or Bredica pacing up and down, detaching the pearls from her crown, the coroana, one after another. Lev didn't see his mother and Bunica meeting the groom's parents, deciding who would do and pay for what. He didn't see his sister get up one night to lay herself down in the snow.

He saw nothing. But he heard the women's voices in the kitchen, the falling pearls, the over-loud laughter of agreement. Heard Bredica's nighttime restlessness, her tread, barefoot this time, the swish of her nightdress, the front door. One night the sounds failed to repeat in reverse, and Lev waited, propped up in bed. He stared into the darkness, deep and dense and full of sounds, listening through the window into the garden and thought he saw his sister, cold as the snow, stretched out just as he lay stretched out, day and night in this bed. Hers was a winter bed, an ice bed, her breathing shallow and steady. The world was perceptible, pin sharp, but out of reach. He was about to call out for his mother when he heard the door, rapid steps, his sister struggling to catch her breath.

Only now did Lev notice his chattering teeth; he pulled the covers over his head, breathed through his mouth and wondered how, in all that time before, he had paid such scant attention to his sister, his brothers, the thousands of sounds, the never-ending soundtrack of bustle, anger, love.

On the day of the wedding, Lev was moved to a stretcher on wheels. Men carried him out, wheeled him up the street to the barn where the wedding was being held. He wasn't wheeled into the church. The church was no place for a bed, said Bunica, which didn't make sense to Lev. When he imagined God, he saw Him lying down, stretched out on one side so He could see what was happening on earth.

He missed the wedding procession, but, propped on a number of cushions, enjoyed the ride. It was good to see the house from outside once more, the yard gate and the bench sitting between decorated beams. Some villagers carried their benches outside, others had fixed benches for two, three or four people; no one else had seating for a dozen. As soon as it got warmer, people sat outside the house, talking, smoking, backs against the wood.

The men wheeled the stretcher up the street, past the neighbours' houses, fences, yard gates. Where the main street met the road to the next village, the houses parted ways. Lev's travelling bed limped over stones and potholes, and cushions and blankets fell off, right outside Fabiu's house. Fabiu of all people: who had set light to tires on midsummer's day, who always won at marbles, Fabiu who had come to visit just once. Cushions and blankets were shaken out and laid back on Lev's stretcher. The snow-drenched cushions made his trousers wet. But once you were on your way, there was no turning back.

The street narrowed, sloping upwards, and Lev looked back once more, as if Fabiu might at any moment appear at the gate, leaning against the house wall, with that slightly upward-travelling look. As if Lev could climb off the stretcher and run to him, and together they would start up the path behind the house until the world turned into hills, undulating, hunch-backed hills rising on all sides until they touched the horizon – mountains and clouds inclining towards one another, like Fabiu and Lev, their words indistinguishable from the sound of the wind over the frozen river.

The advantage of a winter wedding was that the food and wedding cake could be prepared days in advance. Plates and glasses were filled without any great fuss, the guests sat at long tables. The bridal table, decorated with woven cloths, stood by the back wall, and crepe garlands folded by the village children spanned the width of the barn. Bredica hardly touched her food. She was wearing a white blouse with lace ruffles, skirt, waistcoat, and leather opinci shoes bound around her feet. Her eyes were rimmed with black kohl. The crown was held in place with a cord, and Lis had plaited her hair artfully. As beautiful as her late mother, the women said.

Bredica received congratulations, and her husband Ion, also in shirt and waistcoat, tucked away the envelopes. She talked to her friends, her absent manner suggesting she had already moved out of their circle. The band played, and Bredica and Ion placed their hands on each other's shoulders and turned in small circles on the dancefloor. Bredica's face softened, the defiant expression vanished.

Lev's stretcher was moved to the side. A spider lowered itself from the barn roof towards his bed, then disappeared through a gap between the boards. The old women in their black headscarves also sat at the side. Little groups formed everywhere, guests gathering, chatting, drinking, children playing. At the centre of the barn, couples danced. Women came up to Lev, stroked his face with rough hands, soft hands, wrinkled hands; he sensed pity, curiosity, reassurance. Two girls from his class came up, and he felt himself being viewed, a curiosity on public display. Lis helped him to the toilet, brought him food and drinks, adjusted the cushions, which Lev didn't want. On this evening, he would have liked to look as if he could manage by himself. He tried to put on an impassive, proud face like his sister. Then it became too much of a strain. The truth was that he was enjoying the evening. He listened to the music (violin, guitar, drum), and took note of all the stories, major and minor, that played out at a wedding. Later he would tell Bredica all about it. He was still collecting stories when he realised he wouldn't be able to. When he got home, she wouldn't be there.

For a long time, whenever Lev thought of his sister he saw only one image, as if it had suppressed all other images of her.

He saw her revolving, her skirt flying, face softening, and he hoped she had found something in her marriage.

Something like happiness, perhaps?

The dance floor filled. Some couples could dance and others just shifted from foot to foot or stood still, bending their upper bodies like reeds in the wind. Someone leapt onto a table, and glasses fell to the floor. It was the groom's father, puffing on a cigar, the smoke wreathing his head rising into a halo. He danced down the line of tables, more crockery hit the floor, and the men clapped, egging him on, while Bunica, evidently neither surprised nor outraged, fetched a broom to sweep up the shards. Amid the chaos, Lev realised someone was missing. His grandfather had not arrived from Transylvania. A week earlier, he had brought his envelope for the bridal couple and visited Lev in his sickbed, with the same reserve he'd shown ever since their trip to the health resort. As far as Lev knew, no one had reproached him since the accident.

Now the groom's father was climbing ponderously down from the table, with none of his former vim (as if descending the face of a mountain whose peaks were obscured by cigar smoke). Bunica proffered the broom handle to steady him. On the dancefloor, men were forming a circle, spinning to the music, overtaking it; the contents of a glass spilled, and Bredica's husband lay laughing on the floor.

His mother and uncle stood deep in conversation to one side, as if the uproar around them did not exist. His late father's brother managed a hotel on the Black Sea coast; he was a tall man with sparing, self-assured gestures and a silver-shadowed beard. He exuded an irrepressible vitality, but also severity, and Lev was always unsure of himself in his presence. He reminded Lev of his father, but lacked the familiar tenderness. His uncle visited rarely. And when he was here, he got into arguments with Valea. Seeing him was painful. If only emotions could be as easily untangled as the knots in Bredica's necklaces.

Two men pushed Lev back home that night. The street must have gained more potholes since their journey out, and eventually his mother decided to carry the blanket rather than bend down every few metres to pick it up. Exposed to the night air, he was holding on with both hands. One of the men said he had to peel off, and as Lev was wondering what that meant, the other disappeared as well. His mother tucked the blanket under him, so tight he could barely move. She leaned on the stretcher, waiting, beginning to grumble. Those bloody drunkards had just abandoned them, she said.

'What do we do now?' Lev asked.

Lis tried to push the travelling bed herself, but gave up when it got wedged a few metres further on.

She started laughing.

'We wait.'

'For what?'

'For someone to find us.'

'What if no one comes?'

Lev wriggled under the blanket until his arm was free.

'Sit down,' he offered.

A glance up the street to make sure, and then she pushed his legs to one side and sat with him. Silence, or what passed for silence at night: the cry of an owl, dogs barking, the rushing river, a laugh from somewhere. The sky was so far away, a domed watch glass covering the stretcher. This was the moment to ask his mother if she believed he would walk again one day. If Bredica would be happy. It was the time to ask whether she missed his father. But these weren't questions in the proper sense, of words and sentences, they were lamentations, the ways his thoughts tended to go, and so they weren't asked. Even in the darkness, even if they didn't have such conversations, he had a clear picture of his mother. That was enough.

Later his uncle and Valea came to get them.

At home, they had realised two people were missing.

Dividing up the day stopped the time becoming boundless. In the morning his mother washed him, shook out the bedclothes, aired the room. Brought him toast sprinkled with sugar, elderflower or rosehip tea. After breakfast a woman came to give him lessons: Aunty Anuţa, who wasn't a real aunt – his own or anyone else's, as far as he knew – but insisted on being addressed as such. Aunty Anuţa brought books, dog-eared old things that must have been over thirty years old. Mathematics and geography, then Romanian grammar and German literature.

Lev studied tables listing the countries of the world, their rivers, mountains, time zones. Discovered how long the railway was in different parts of the world, learned about solids and liquids, gases, fuels, speeds, forgot some of it immediately, but remembered the Beaufort wind scale: Two = light breeze. Four = moves small branches. Six = whistling in telegraph wires. Eight = whole trees in motion. Ten to twelve = hurricane.

Sometimes he wondered what the rest of his class was learning, and whether he would ever manage to fit back in.

Twice a week a woman came from the next village. She was someone his grandmother knew, and just laid her hands on him. She laid them on his knee, slid them under his bottom, touched his collar bone. At first, he found her touch unpleasant. The way her hands roamed over his body, settling here and there until the spot grew warm, felt too intimate. He closed his eyes, not wanting to know if she was staring at him, not wanting to see anything, neither her face nor the downy hair above her lip.

People with freckles were oversensitive, she said. You had to find the right pressure for the treatment to work, not too hard, not too gentle. Lev didn't understand what that had to do with his freckles, but he didn't argue.

'Don't screw your face up,' she said.

'Sorry?'

'I can see you screwing your face up. Relax.'

Lev relaxed. And found that her hands could be on his legs and his scalp could tingle at the same time. As if everything was connected.

The worst part of the day, which had once been the nicest, began with an afternoon nap. There was nothing to fill the afternoon and slice it up. Life moved through the house, the garden, the village streets; Lev listened for footsteps, voices, silence. He filled them out with his imagination, and now and then someone did come into the room, his mother, his grandmother, neighbours. Bredica, who used to look in several times a day, now came only rarely. The noises from the kitchen grew louder, and his mother brought food and lit a candle. Shadows lengthened; his thoughts stretched out. If he was lucky, he might sleep for several hours before waking again.

In the morning, he was relieved to have got through another night, begun another day; one night and one day fewer – fewer than what? Could you measure this business? Was he required to wait out this time in order to be part of life again later? Once you had dropped out, were you always a dropout, always on the margins?

Reluctant to be pinned down, the doctor said little. Lev had the impression that he didn't know what was wrong with his patient, or for that matter what could be done for him. He held himself erect, entered the room with a measured tread and swung his doctor's bag up, only to brake a few centimetres from the table, setting the bag down quite gently, almost without a noise, as if this was his first trick. The second consisted of all manner of examinations, shining a light in Lev's eyes, bending and stretching his knee, and finding nothing, neither what was wrong nor how to help Lev, though he did present a bill for this. For nothing and nothing again. For the trick of making a bag fly through the room.

At the start of December his teacher visited, to see how he was getting on with schoolwork. Realising that he was being taught (in her words) using books from the last century, she decided that from then on, someone would bring him exercises to complete.

That someone was Kato.

Lev assured her that Aunty Anuța had other books – there

was no need to send Kato. And he thought: no, no, please not that. How could it be that everything just kept getting worse? Wasn't it bad enough that he had to lie here, that Fabiu didn't visit, his grandfather scarcely came and Bredica had moved out? Now he would have to put up with this girl every afternoon. The other children shunned her. Most teachers ignored her, never called on her – it was only his class teacher who had developed an inexplicable liking for her. Lev spoke to his mother, asking her to take the work from the girl at the door, to spare him.

For the first time since he had lost the use of his legs, Lis flew into a rage.

'Spare *me*!'

Since when had he become so conceited as to think himself better than this girl?

She came the very next day. The yard gate opened, the dog barked then quietened down surprisingly fast, footsteps approached. His mother went to the door and greeted the girl, brought her into the room. Lev tried to look as indifferent as possible. Kato's eyes roamed over everything before settling on him. They nodded to each other. Then she sat down on the chair that had been pulled up near the bed for her. He knew his face gave him away; he caught a warning glance from his mother. Couldn't they have sent a boy? Or, if it had to be a girl, then one from the front row. If a front row girl was sitting here, he would make an effort to understand the work. If one of them came, these would be hours he would look forward to impatiently. Instead, they had sent this girl, shunned by everyone. Who was always scribbling something on a sheet of paper at break time; so absent you might think she wasn't capable of speech. But whenever she was asked a question in class, she knew the answer. That was surprising. He thought her snooty. Or stupid.

Maybe both.

The house where she and her father lived lay on a side street off the road out of the village. The fence was low, pickets stuck in the earth at angles like loose teeth. Behind it lay the unsecured yard, and a wooden house with doors that stood open in warm months. A smashed window had been patched up with cardboard and a picture of the Eiffel Tower. Overgrown currants, gooseberries, raspberries; no flowers or trees, apart from a single pear tree. A swing hung from the thickest branch. Almost every time he passed, the girl was on the swing. She twisted the ropes tight and then surrendered herself to the spinning, eyes closed.

Winding. Unwinding.

Sometimes he felt sorry for her. Her mother was said to have died a few months after she was born. Her father couldn't care less whether Kato's hair (which couldn't decide if it wanted to be straight or curly) was combed, if her face was washed, if her clothes had holes. She had surprisingly pale eyes and a laugh that strayed into joy only at the edges.

When he walked past her fence, they would nod to one another. A look, a nod, deliberate indifference as he walked on, as she went on turning beneath the tree. He had always walked on, even when he felt like hiding behind the nearest bush to watch her. Did she spend all afternoon dangling from those ropes?

Sitting in bed with the back rest raised, Lev punished Kato with feigned disinterest, as if all this was her fault, and yet: when she'd entered the room, they had nodded to one another just as they did over the fence. They sat in silence until Lis arrived with tea. His mother touched Kato's shoulder, and her head inclined towards the touch.

'Have you brought something for Lev?'

Kato, her mouth full of sweet tea, handed Lev several sheets of paper.

'These are the exercises.'

Her tongue brushed very softly against her teeth.

Lev flicked through the papers.

Kato read his expression correctly. She pulled the chair up to the bed and explained the work. Lev had assumed she would have a pungent smell. But the scent he caught was milk and something floating, light, like a clear morning.

'He doesn't even try. Lies in his room staring at the wall. And yet he gets fed three times a day. How much longer?'

These words from his eldest brother felt like a knife in his chest. He didn't hear his mother's response; she spoke too quietly. The 'how much longer' rang in his ears. How much longer – until what? Would they take him into the mountains and leave him there, or slip him under the ice in the Iza? Would he feel a pillow over his face one night? His brother might not move as quietly as Bredica, but he was strong. Lev would fight back, or perhaps he wouldn't – he might just lie there, stretched out, and accept the darkness that was already his home. His mother and sister would miss him. The house would miss having someone listening to it. But Kato would be saved from having to drop in on the cripple every afternoon, a slow-witted boy to boot. She would be glad.

Now Lev slept even less, waking with a start, thinking someone had crept into his room with a pillow in their hands. He grew paler, thinner, and saw the change reflected in his mother's face, which was his mirror. The doctor said he needed fresh air and change, though he wasn't to move – the shock of what he'd been through had not yet been processed – and Lev almost burst out laughing. It was January, would they put his bed out in the garden? Who had the will and the time to organise a change? The doctor asked if anyone could get hold of petrol; if they could, he would consult a colleague who was an expert in paralysis brought on by nervous disorders.

When his mother brought food, Lev tried to smile. When she shook out his bedclothes, changed the chamber pot, washed him with quick, practised movements, he laid his hand on hers. It was meant as thanks, but his mother wept.

At some point it became almost impossible to tell days from nights; they could be discerned only from their margins. Light appearing at the window, a draught of air, words he didn't understand, bread he couldn't chew, soup he couldn't swallow. Only water still tasted delicious. His mother took his food away untouched.

The limits of his body began to blur. Where did skin end and the bed begin? The room gave way under his weight. He was sinking. In the dark, everything that gave purchase was gone, everything that showed which way was up and which down, where his body was in space. He was lying on a bed, but maybe he was also floating down a river, or falling through the water, ever deeper.

Kato brought schoolwork, but Lev lay still, apathetic, understanding and saying nothing. Kato left and came back the next day. She didn't go through the exercises, just sat by his bed, drawing or reading aloud to him. He could barely follow her, but didn't want her to stop.

In Lev's dreams his legs were there, letting him walk wherever he wanted. Into the past, the future. He took every path. He walked through the village, greeted people, walked with them a little way. Have you seen him? Who? The man with the round hat. He walks down the street, knocking on every door. He carries a little lamb, his waistcoat is turning red. No one opens the door to him. Take a little more cloud to go with that, there, where the hills are. The grass is tall, no one is mowing, no one is binding it into stacks. The wind reaches between these stalks. The ice on the Iza cracks, breaks up, and the water overflows the banks, taking away the winter, washing Lev out into the countryside.

It was my brother, Mama, in the night.

The little lamb is dead.

The doctor had been. Lev had missed the trick with the bag. He became aware of the man only when he shone a light in Lev's eyes. The doctor's face was expressionless, his mouth moved. Told to raise his arm, he stretched it sideways. For a while now he had been lost in space, not knowing which way was up, if he was lying or falling. Lev closed his eyes, and when he opened them again the doctor had gone. A candle was burning in a cup, and his mother spoke his whole Christian name, in three syllables, like a question.

The forest whispered, here was cloud-white. He counted noiselessly behind a tree, nine, eight, seven, six… Where was everyone? Spring days, storks' nests, apple trees in blossom, baked doughnuts (filled with jam that runs over your fingers), half-forgotten scenes: a smile, hands made of light, a grey sheepskin waistcoat, chalk clouds on the blackboard, a face turned away, patiently waiting, the slack, flayed skin of a steer, the smell of the cattle market, the feeling of bare feet sinking into a cowpat, crackling hay. Pictures lined up one after another, and they were enough; he had no need to get up, could lose himself in these memories, going through the whole thing again, experiencing every thing, every single day. He felt hot, wrestled with the covers, pushed them off the bed, began to shiver, called out for his mother, for Bredica. Where was everyone?

He had to provide the nuts.

He mustn't throw the stone.

No one was at home.

Everyone – not just his family but the whole village – was at the river, laden with jugs, bottles, buckets. The priest would plunge the cross into the river three times: asJesus had been baptised in the Jordan, every single body of water was holy, every stream, every river, including the Iza. His grandmother kept the consecrated water until the next Epiphany, beside the picture of the Virgin Mary in her bedroom. If a cow was in calf, if someone was sick, she fetched it. Now she would probably use it on Lev.

Because the Iza was frozen, they had to hammer a hole in the ice to dip the cross. People might be chilled to the bone, but no one showed impatience, even if it took a long time; they would stand there, shifting their weight from one leg to the other, beneath flags and feast-day icons, listening to the voice of the pope, even if they were too far away to hear.

That morning, Lev's mind was unusually clear; he had slept for several hours at a stretch, even eaten some of the semolina porridge his mother had brought him, with cinnamon and honey. He listened to the silence of the house as it merged into the silence of the village. No one stayed away from this ceremony, if they could walk. Was that a sound? The gate opening, the front door, footsteps in the hallway – he held his breath. Had someone come back early, one of his brothers? The dog hadn't barked. The door of his room was pushed open by one foot, as if someone had their hands full. Lev's heart pounded; he couldn't even get out 'who's there?', and the person on the other side of the threshold didn't speak, either, but waited in silence until the door had swung open.

It was Kato. Holding a tabby cat in her arms.

They'd had a visitor, said Kato: a friend of her late mother had dropped by with a wagon full of animals. He'd even had a rattlesnake. The tomcat had an impressive pedigree, she said, and his name was Khalil, which was Arabic for 'good friend'.

Lev had his doubts about the story; Khalil looked like a normal cat to him. There were a lot of cats in the village. Someone might take care of the lucky ones, give them milk, let them sit by the stove in winter. Others had to fend for themselves, look for food, hunt or live half-feral in the woods. Kato stuck to her story. Khalil was of noble blood, and she had known at once that he was meant for Lev (well, he could use a friend, couldn't he?). The cat's demeanour came as confirmation. He wriggled free of Kato's arms and, after taking a good look around, jumped onto the bed. He brushed slowly past Lev's legs, reached his chest, sniffed his neck and stared at him. Lev had never looked a cat in the eye at such close range. Khalil's eyes were rimmed in black lines that continued along the grain of the fur to his back. His rainbow skin was grey-green with black flecks, his fur tabby-brown, his throat and paws white, as if he was wearing boots. There was no smile in the animal's eyes, but no fear, either. Unfathomable depth and seriousness.

Only his mother knew about Khalil. The cat came and went without anyone noticing. He would wait in the loggia until someone opened the door, then slip inside. Lev never knew when Khalil would return, but if the cat had been away for several hours, he found himself waiting for him.

Khalil brought the cold of the snow, then in the unusually warm spring, the sun on his fur. He brought the excitement of the hunt, exhaustion, hunger – and although Lev was now sharing his food with the cat, he started to regain weight. Khalil wasn't choosy. He would even eat bread and butter or polenta.

Lev admired the way he could move without making a sound. He didn't hear the cat enter the room, only felt the pressure of his paws, the weight of Khalil's body on his own. To his surprise he discovered that the animal never smelled; he seemed to have no scent of his own. His fur was always clean, even his paws. After his patrols, Khalil came into the room, leapt onto the bed, formed a perfect circle on Lev's legs or lengthened himself into a streamlined shape, and slept.

Lev never tired of watching his changing positions. Since he couldn't feel his legs, they couldn't go numb. They lay like that for hours without moving, Lev watching over Khalil as he slept.

The cries woke him. They were part of the night like barking dogs, calling owls. Until now, they had been no concern of his, but now he listened, tense, his whole body an extension of his ears. Lev called for his mother, and she was soon at his side, in her nightshirt, hair in a plait that went down to her chest.

'Khalil,' he said.

His mother didn't seem to understand.

'He needs help.'

His mother sat on his bed. Her expression was tired, indulgent.

'He'll manage without us,' she said. 'A cat knows when it's worth fighting, and when it isn't.'

They both listened to the outside world, but there was nothing more to be heard.

'Do you?' She looked at him.

Lev pretended not to know what she meant.

'Do you know that, too?'

He had no idea what he could do, said Lev.

'You could talk to me about it.'

Lev turned his face away. He didn't want to remember. Lonja's body in the basin, twisted and loose, as if she had run towards death, only seeing who it was at the last moment.

He should have been faster, said Lev. If he'd been faster, she might still be alive.

But how was this his fault, Lis asked. She called him 'My darling boy,' as she used to. He was not to blame for the accident – he had tried to help, and he wasn't to persuade himself that that had been wrong.

Lev's legs began to twitch. He didn't want his mother to see and asked her to open the window a crack.

'You'll be cold,' Lis objected.

'Please.'

She brought him another blanket and opened the window. Lev listened to the night. A stream of air chilled his face, a scrabbling sound, then nothing for a long time, until the corrugated iron outside the window creaked and he felt the familiar weight on his body. Khalil came to Lev's face, pressed his nose against Lev's, a damp, surprising coldness; Lev lifted the covers and Khalil lay down, his head close to Lev's neck. It was the first time he had stroked the cat.

The next morning Lev discovered Khalil's face was scratched and one paw bloodied.

Kato visited every afternoon, they read texts in German and Romanian, and studied tables and equations the purpose of which Lev was slow to grasp.

They'd had a speech therapist in school, Kato told him, who checked that all the children were rolling their Rs.

'Rică nu ştia să zică: rău, răţuşca, rămurică.'

'Do yours roll?' she asked.

Lev repeated, rău, răţuşca, rămurică.

Kato tilted her head benevolently.

'Your tongue doesn't roll when you speak German.'

Lev said: Straße, Trauben, Radieschen.

Kato repeated the words; Radieschen was the only one she didn't manage first time.

'I wish they'd teach us something useful,' said Lev.

Kato's eyes were sympathetic, but she said nothing. Lev couldn't work out why this girl, of all people, could grasp everything so effortlessly. She would make a good teacher herself one day. When he told her that, she shook her head, and Lev felt shame, thinking of all the breaktimes she had spent alone. That no one went up to her, that even the teachers for the most part ignored her had felt right to him, as if that was just the way things were. Who'd choose to go back to school if they were treated like that? Or was it something else?

Lev handed Kato a little box that had been sitting on his bedside table. She opened the lid, looked at the contents for a while, and then pinned the mărțișor pendant on its red and white cord to her jumper. She didn't say anything. But when she said goodbye, she gave him a kiss.

One morning Lev was woken by the sound of a whiplash. The shepherd was walking through the village, bringing out the flock. Lev was excited by the familiar noise, but Khalil didn't like it. He stared in the direction it was coming from and disappeared before he could be reassured. He probably slipped through the door when Dorin went to let the cows out of the cowshed.

Lev looked forward to breakfast, to the spring, to the day. Above all, he looked forward to Kato. For some time now he had known that she didn't see the daily visit as a chore. She came smiling into the room where he was waiting for her, combed and washed, sometimes with and sometimes without Khalil, whom she treated with the polite indifference the cat preferred. Lev liked her voice, her smile, and began trying to make her laugh. It almost always worked, and once, when they had laughed about something together, she asked him why he couldn't walk any more.

Lev told her about the accident. Suddenly, it was almost easy. He felt like he was under a spell, he said, as if he could never escape what he'd seen.

Animals sometimes played dead until the danger had passed, said Kato.

He'd never thought of that. For some time now, his legs had been twitching. At night in particular they were gripped by uncontrollable spasms. On a few occasions they felt cold, or itchy, but he said nothing to his mother, not wanting to get her hopes up. He went over and over what had happened, trying to find a way out – Lonja and Silas's argument, losing sight of them, finding them again, and the man ordering him to stay where he was.

'The danger has passed,' said Kato, and it sounded like a fact. He tried to object, but she brushed his words aside.

'Doesn't your father say anything when you stay out all night?'

From the movement of her head, Lev could tell that Kato was saying no.

Stars appeared, one after another, as if someone was directing a secret light show. There was nothing, nothing beyond the stars, a neighbour had once told Lev, and that firm 'nothing' had frightened him. How could there be nothing beyond the stars? But the neighbour said that some events snuffed out all faith; he was just too young to understand.

Why did adults think you were too young to understand something, then say it anyway? And when you wanted to know more, they wouldn't tell you.

Kato said she often stayed out when her father was travelling with his bee colonies. In summer she slept in the garden, or sometimes in one of the mountain huts.

'Aren't you scared, on your own in the mountains?'

'I was born on a Saturday,' said Kato, as if that was an explanation. Then: 'Children born on a Saturday are lucky. My mother said that.'

He didn't ask how she could know.

Kato lay next to him like a plank. He made himself narrow, she made herself narrow, they couldn't both be comfortable, plus he was semi exposed as she had taken most of the covers for herself. But lying here was even lovelier than he had imagined. This was why he had asked for the rolling stretcher to be set up in the garden. The request was denied, of course, but he hadn't given up, and finally one mild evening Dorin and his mother wheeled the bed out onto the grass between the vegetable plot and hen house. Beyond the animal stalls lay the grass, and beyond the grass lay hills, then mountains – and beyond that something else.

Kato was wearing a shawl Lis had knitted for her. Her hair was tied back, her eyes like silken wings in the dark. Khalil leapt onto the bed, forced his way between their legs.

'Now we really can't move,' said Lev.

'Who wants to.'

In his dream, he was at the river. The edges were still iced over, thin layers with water pulsing beneath. Ducks, swans and countless birds nested on the bank. They didn't move, were perhaps asleep. The silence of this scene was more than the absence of noise, it was a great listening, an awaiting. The river was listening for something, so were the plants and animals. This listening went right through Lev, through his chest, his belly, his legs, lasting barely longer than a few breaths then it lay behind him and was gone. The ducks raised their heads from under their wings. Birds took flight.

Lev felt Khalil jump off the stretcher.

He saw a shadow, recognised his brother.

'What are you doing here?'

A laugh was the only reply.

Kato was being dragged off the stretcher.

He just had to check if she really was a girl, said Valea, clearly drunk.

She knew how to defend herself; that was what really frightened Lev. His helplessness turned to anger, and he uttered terrible threats against his brother. His legs slipped off the stretcher, two thin branches holding up too large a weight. Lev trembled, clinging on with both hands so as not to fall. But he felt grass beneath his feet, cool, firm earth.

He didn't have to do anything more. Say anything.

The pair let go of each other and stared at him.

מְנֵ֥א מְנֵ֖א תְקֵ֥ל וּפַרְסִֽין

Two

• • • • •

The car stopped without warning. Blowing in through the open door, the wind whirled up papers on the back seat, it brushed Lev's face, and he closed his eyes for a moment. Long car journeys made him feel sick. And apart from that, this expanse of land was disturbing, these roads straight as a die, electricity masts in the fields, a vast, grey sky, no clouds, no hills, no mountains.

Ferry had had a good look in all directions before vanishing into the fields. He soon returned with a sunflower head, which he pressed into Lev's hands. Then he started the car and drove on. Lev held the sunflower head like a ball someone had thrown, until his grandfather laughed and told him to eat. It took skill to prise the seeds from the husks; Lev cracked the seeds, wound the window down and spat the husks into the wind. A few blew straight back into the car; these he gathered discreetly in the footwell.

At regular intervals, Ferry held out an open hand and Lev placed sunflower seeds in it. Ferry cracked them quickly, expertly, spitting the husks out of the window as the wind tousled hair worn a little longer than other men. Lev decided to work from the edge towards the centre, eating the outermost circle first, then the second, speeding up as the seed circles grew smaller; he forgot to feel sick, forgot to think about the absence of hills and mountains, and before he reached the centre they had arrived at their destination: Buziaş.

His grandfather paid no heed to Lev's ability to keep up. Everyone else was strolling, lingering on paths and benches. Having reported to reception and received their room key, laden with luggage, Ferry and Lev strode through the park and the colonnade, along a hallway and up flights of stairs until they reached their room.

Ferry checked the bathroom, the condition of the beds, looked inside the wardrobe, ran a finger over the windowsill, flicked lights on and off, straightened the curtains, stepped onto the balcony where he adjusted the furniture and, satisfied, began to unpack. Lev did likewise. He was allocated the lower shelves of the wardrobe, the bottom drawer of the chest, the bed by the window. When everything was put away, clothes in the wardrobe, books on the bedside table, writing things on the desk, wash bag in the bathroom, Ferry got changed. Lev changed, too – it was always best to do as his grandfather did and not ask too many questions.

In a fresh shirt, hair combed and face washed, Ferry seemed transformed. His movements slowed, his breathing calmed, and the steep crease between his eyebrows disappeared. He sat on the edge of the bed, inhaled and exhaled a few times. Lev sat on his own bed and breathed.

Then he heard Ferry clap his hands together.

'Now,' he said. 'Now we're here!'

Being here meant: the feel of the underwear his mother had packed against his skin; the smell of chlorine in the windowless bathroom, muffled voices from adjoining rooms, footsteps overhead made by genteel, dustless shoes; it meant sun in the branches outside the balcony, the thin fabric of the bedclothes and a pressure in his belly which might have had something to do with all the sunflower seeds; it meant restless, meandering thoughts because the days ahead lay unwritten; it meant following his grandfather in two senses, both going where he went and doing what he said; being among people he didn't know, some of whose languages he didn't understand – now he was here, for a week's health cure. He'd been delighted to accompany his grandfather, but he no longer knew why.

Being here also meant not being there.

The sun had set, but the sky was a cloudless blue.

On the way to the main building, Ferry explained that the two hundred plane trees were from Italy and the roofed walkway half a kilometre long. Even on rainy days, you could stroll in the open air. This had been the idea of Emperor Franz Joseph I of Austria, who had come here with Crown Prince Franz Ferdinand and Empress Elisabeth at the end of the nineteenth century.

A man greeted them quietly as they passed. In a whisper, Ferry told Lev not to be surprised if some of the spa guests seemed reserved, or downright impolite. Most lived a secluded life, on account of their ailments. You must never ask a guest about their illness, and you must absolutely never say someone wasn't looking well today.

At the entrance to the dining room, Ferry held him back. 'We wait to be seated.' And soon a waiter arrived, took their names, consulted his list and led them to a table. As they crossed the large hall, weaving between the round tables, Ferry continued his explanations: the table was important, he said, the most important thing in fact, because your dining companions determined the course of your stay. You met three times a day for meals, and experience showed that connections made at the table were consolidated beyond it. The people you sat with would speak to you on walks, at exercise classes, in the changing rooms, in the baths – that's right, even when you were lying in the tub, eyes closed, they would accost you. And you just had to put up with these people, unless someone left; that was the only way company was reshuffled. He had been reshuffled both upwards and downwards in his time, but it seldom improved matters. If they were seated with people who droned on about their ailments all evening, then God help them. Or with couples newly in love, even worse. No, the worst was couples who had long since fallen out of love. He was hoping for interesting guests, perhaps a scientist or an artist. Or pensioners with whom he could play chess. Was Lev hoping for anyone in particular?

Lev was confused. Before he could say anything, they had reached their table. Six people raised their heads and looked at them inquisitively.

No one spoke about their condition. Lev took this as a good sign for the week. A few knew each other already. A couple from Timişoara who introduced themselves as the Radus had already spent several evenings at this table with two sisters from Braşov. Today's other new arrivals were a stand-offish young man (an artist, perhaps) and an older lady whose crutches were hooked over the back of her chair.

Lev looked around. There was no other child his age. Waiters moved between the tables, obliging but not especially friendly. The lights were overly bright, illuminating every corner of the hall. The guests chatted, though some, like him, were examining the others with curiosity. His grandfather had made the acquaintance of the sister to his left, filled her glass (as he would continue to do all evening, unasked) and then began a conversation across the table with Mr Radu. Conversation wasn't quite the right word, it was more of an interrogation. How had the weather been these last few days? What was the water quality like this year? Was the new bottling plant any good? Was this or that therapist still working there? Had the paths been repaired? Was the cinema operating?

After the soup, Ferry launched into a lecture on galvanic baths. A galvanic bath relieved pain and rheumatic inflammation, improved circulation and thus helped to flush out toxins. The flow of electricity through the body had to be carefully calibrated, however; as ladies were present, he would not describe his suffering in detail. At this point the sisters exchanged a glance, and Mr Radu used the interruption to turn and speak to his wife. Determined not to take offence, Ferry pressed on, paying no heed to the fact that the only people listening were Lev and the lady with the crutches. He closed by saying that alongside the therapeutic massages, the galvanic baths were the best thing this resort had to offer.

A dull thud. The jolt went right through him. The car came off the road, careened into the field at full speed. They were plunged into shadow, dark suns scraped at the windows. Stalks snapped, drumming against metal, the car was slowing. He was sitting in the passenger seat beside his grandfather; Lev turned round, three laughing women sat in the back seat. He put his hands over his ears.

Beyond the field lay a village. Built into a steep cliff, stone-grey walls, brightly coloured shutters at the windows, some striped, others with painted designs. Twilight already. 'Hurry up!' cried Ferry, shooing him up a street with the luggage. Lev turned, the women had gone. They stopped outside a house, the door opened by itself and on the threshold, he felt something holding him back.

At night, all the shutters on the lakeside had to be closed. That was the only thing that mattered, his grandfather said. Got it? On cue, one domino toppling the next, the shutters in all the houses started closing. Leaning out, Lev watched the wave of shutters and with perfect timing fitted his window into the pattern. It was dark inside now, Ferry was searching for the light switch, when the screaming started.

Someone forced Lev into a wooden tub. Electrodes were lowered into the water, a tingling spread over his skin, a bright flicker in his eyes. 'Stay calm,' someone said, 'it'll soon be over.' A thin layer of copper was already forming on his body, a second, clinging skin that covered him entirely. He was lifted out of the water and set down on his feet, stiff and heavy; an effort to bend his legs and turn his head. He raised his hands, counted ten copper fingers, looked down – his body shone like a reflective window pane.

In the morning, it took Lev a while to shake off the copper skin from his dream. He kept checking his hands. In the glaring light of the bathroom, something seemed to shine for a moment.

Ferry was in the habit of singing in the morning. He sang as he washed, as he dressed, was still singing as he locked the door. The first thing he said on the way to the main building was that after breakfast, they had an appointment with the chief physician.

'Me too?' Lev asked.

'Yes, of course.'

They met again at the table. The Radus, Silas (Lev and Ferry called him 'the artist') and the lady with the crutches. The sisters from Braşov were the last to arrive. Both were in their early twenties, and obviously related. The older sister had a serious face and short hair, while the younger was a little shorter, wore her hair long and smiled at Lev as they sat down. No one crossed themselves before eating. No one said grace. They began when they wanted, stopped when they wanted and, above all, ate whatever they wanted. That first morning, Lev restricted himself to bread and honey, and watery-tasting milk.

Conversation circled around the new arrivals' appointments with the chief physician. Mr Radu assured them with great authority that the doctor was very young and had to be helped along a bit. He advised the newcomers to consider in advance which therapies they considered vital. The chief physician was on an economy drive, and they would no longer be given the best as a matter of course, as in previous years. He had managed to obtain massages, magnetic field therapy and herbal baths for both himself and his wife, he said, adding the words 'every day'. At these, his audience finally responded in the desired manner. Mr Radu must have resolved not to leave the floor entirely to Lev's grandfather.

Several times, Ferry attempted to carve himself a slice of the conversation. He spoke of the weather, then the inadequate lighting in the corridors, but every advance was parried. Radu had commandeered breakfast for himself.

The one person taking absolutely no interest in this was the artist. He looked like he had slept badly. Perhaps he too had been galvanised.

Was it surprise Lev saw on the face of the chief physician? Mockery? Tedium? Then a studied smile, a practised gesture, somewhere between beckoning and dismissal. He was dressed in white. White trousers, white top, white coat. Lev had never been to see a doctor. His heart pounded and he didn't know where to put himself. A plant in urgent need of water was the only decoration in this austere room; the desk held piles of journals and books, and a typewriter. A poster of Ceaușescu hung on the wall.

'Do take a seat,' said the doctor, and Lev sat on an examination table. Instantly, his bare calves stuck to it. Without further questions, the doctor began to examine him. He looked in his ears, listened to his heart, looked down his throat, shone a light in his eyes. No one had ever looked in Lev's ears, throat or any other place. Lev tried to decipher the name embroidered on the white coat, but the letters wouldn't join up. He submitted, closed his eyes, raised his arm, turned his head, pulled up his shirt.

'Does this hurt?' the doctor asked, pressing his belly in different places.

Lev shook his head, even when it did.

'And this?'

Lev answered with a firm 'No.'

The room was silent for a spell, and Lev assumed the examination was over. Ceauşescu looked benevolent, grandfatherly, his gleaming hair and black suit contrasting with the blue-yellow-red flag. He'd never understood why the left-hand side of the poster showed scaffolding rising into the sky. His brother Valea said it represented progress. Was progress a scaffold?

The examination table made a sucking noise as he got up. The doctor wrote something on a slip of paper. He signalled with a nod that the patient was free to go. Lev seized the note hastily and it was completely crumpled when he handed it to the secretary. The secretary copied the words onto a pad of light blue, thick, almost square paper.

The wind was strong. The flowers bent their heads to the ground. As if the wind, too, was asking: does this hurt?

Hedges lined the paths, twigs protruding here and there like searching feelers. Lev sat on a bench, put the unread therapy timetable beside him and weighted it with a stone. He couldn't stop marvelling at the plane trees. How would they feel beside the spruces and firs of the Maramureş? But what did they see all day? People strolling about, pale, tired.

Someone sat beside him, and only on a second glance did

he recognise one of the sisters from Braşov. Her eyes were blue, blue-shadowed with something Lev couldn't name. Her nose was narrow, perhaps a little crooked, but that didn't bother him. A gold necklace gleamed in her decolletage. During the communal meals she had been just one of the many people suddenly in his field of vision. Now she was beside him, and the realisation that she was beautiful took him unawares.

'I'm Helene, but everyone calls me Lonja.'

'I'm Leonhard, but they call me Lev.'

'Like the lion?'

'Yes.'

She asked to see his timetable, scanned the lines, slid the paper back under the stone.

Suddenly he felt her hand on his leg.

'Look!'

Two squirrels were bounding across the grass, swift and weightless. They took a look around, then sprang up a tree, disappearing into the leaves. Lev couldn't tell whether his elation came from the sight of the animals or the gentle pressure on his thigh.

'You need to come here at sunset,' said Lonja. 'Then the whole lawn will be full of them.'

Her eyebrows were two thin arches. Her complexion was light, the skin almost translucent. Only now did it strike Lev that they had spoken German together quite naturally.

Eventually she got up.

'Lonja?' called Lev.

She turned.

'Did it say anything about galvanic baths?'

His grandfather studied their therapy timetables on the balcony. Ferry always booked a room with a balcony as he liked to smoke after meals. He smoked with a cigarette holder, because it was healthier, and owned an etui with a built-in watch mechanism that released just one cigarette every four hours.

From here, buildings, paths, benches and plane trees looked like a drawing made with the lightest strokes. People didn't seem to move, they were screwed down into their positions, and Lev couldn't help being reminded of the girl in his class who drew pictures every breaktime. Once he had crept up behind her, and although she clearly noticed, she'd pretended he wasn't there. She was sketching a tree, right down to the thinnest branches. Lev didn't know much about art, but the drawing was beautiful. He'd said nothing. Just as he never said anything when he walked past her house and saw her on the swing in the pear tree. When she wasn't in the garden, he was tempted to go back and wait for her.

Without the girl, something was missing.

Ferry struck a match, and the skin of his cupped hand glowed pink.

In summary, it was walks and herbal baths, and a recommendation to take the waters. Lev was relieved. That sounded harmless, though he didn't know why he needed a cure at all, he wasn't sick. You don't have to be sick for a health cure, said Ferry. The cure was to stop you getting sick, and there was nowhere better than here. His own schedule looked more extensive. Would they see each other at all, except for meals?

Ferry stretched his legs, slipping into an indolent pose.

He only did that when he smoked; the rest of the time he sat impeccably upright.

'I wonder why the Radus are here.'

Lev shrugged, though no answer was expected of him.

'For the wife, my bet would be a psychological complaint. Him, I'm not sure about. Some problem with his oesophagus, perhaps.'

Ferry took a drag, sliding further down into his chair.

'The lady with the crutches, what's her name, Rosina something – that's clear enough. Polio in childhood, resulting in a disorder of the musculoskeletal system. With our artist, things are more complicated. A disease of the airways or the heart. Yes, it could be his heart.'

'You mean he has a weak heart?'

'I mean he's lovesick,' said Ferry.

'And the sisters?'

'I can't tell with the older one; for the younger, I would say an asthenic neurosis.'

Lev tried to look as if he understood a word of this.

At lunchtime, the sky turned dark in minutes. Rain began to fall. Thanks to Emperor Franz Joseph they were able to walk part of the way under the colonnade. The plane trees rustled, men hurried past with umbrellas, women in crackling rain capes. They were out of breath when they reached the Grand Hotel, having run the final, unroofed stretch of the way.

In the brightly lit dining room Lonja looked so alone that Lev had an urge to sit next to her. But seating arrangements were not alterable unless someone left or someone arrived.

They smiled at each another across the table. Ferry noticed this private sign and raised quizzical eyebrows, while Lev turned his attention to the arrangement of plate, cutlery and napkin.

At last the party was fully assembled at their table, soup was served, and Lonja talked to her sister, casting only an occasional glance at Silas – who, like Lev, was secretly watching her. Lev wanted to say something to her but erred on the side of caution, staying silent throughout the meal.

The rain grew heavier, trees bent outside. Bushes pressed against the glass as if asking to be let in. Then a sudden boom, and the lights went out. A whisper ran around the room; someone cried out.

Gradually, candles were brought in, and the dining hall became a vast space whose edges were lost in blackness. Lonja's shoulders were swallowed by her dark jumper; only her face and hands stood out.

'A melancholy rumble, dully-deep; / The sky's dark lashes blink with all their might, / As eyes will blink before they start to weep – / And, glimpsed beneath those lashes, feeble light. / Now from the fens the chilly showers creep / And quiet fog across the common land; / While brooding on its grief, the sky lets slip / The sun, a ball dropped from a careless hand.'

The artist had recited a poem into the silence. Lonja's luminous hands lay motionless on the table; her eyes were closed. Then she turned her head to Silas. A look defenceless in its openness.

Mr Radu requested a translation into the national language.

This was a poem by Lenau, Ferry explained. It wasn't easy to translate.

What was so difficult about it, Mr Radu asked, after all, Lenau was a Romanian poet.

'Not at all,' Ferry shot back. 'Lenau wrote in German, so he's a German poet.' Turning to the sisters, he added, how on earth was one supposed to translate 'dully-deep', for example.

Mr Radu said something about renaming and the commune of Lenauheim, then refrained from further objections, quite possibly because of the pacifying gesture from his wife.

'When Lenau was born, the Banat belonged to Hungary and was part of the Habsburg Empire,' Silas said. 'Lenau is neither a German nor a Romanian poet; he's Austrian.'

Afternoon nap.

Afternoon naps meant coming in from the street, stopping what you were doing, even if something crucial was about to happen, in games of football or marbles. Lev had to undress down to his underpants and get into bed, closed window shutters letting in just enough light to reveal the shapes of the furniture.

This ritual derived from Ferry. After lunch you had to rest, whether you were alone or had visitors. You very rarely slept; everyone lingered instead in thought, though sometimes they pretended to sleep– or really did. There was no telling.

It was a stolen hour; anyone who knocked on the door was sent away, and jobs that needed doing were laid aside. It was as though the day had a pause, a third space alongside day and night, and they stepped into this space together. Sometimes

Lev's mother undressed to her slip and lay down beside him. Bredica and Dorin joined the afternoon nap, too; perhaps the friction between Lev and Valea was because they never shared that hour. At some point you just got too old. Ferry could only take a nap when his daughter was very young; later he had too much work on the watch glasses, and also she was too big and he didn't want to lie beside her. But Lis only stopped getting under the bedclothes with her friends when she left school. When her father came to wake them, the girls told him things they might never have said otherwise.

Lev was thinking about what he was. If that question was so difficult for Lenau, then how was it for him?

A rustle told him his grandfather had woken from his 'noppen' (his name for a sleep during an afternoon rest), and Lev asked him: well then, what was he?

A few deep breaths from the other bed. When you had a Transylvanian Saxon mother, a Romanian father and an Austrian grandfather, it wasn't a simple matter.

Lev had never understood why his grandfather was Austrian.

'My father was from Vienna, my mother from Sighişoara. Have I not told you that?'

Lev shook his head, which of course Ferry couldn't see.

A few minutes passed, and then Ferry sat up. He said that when things were as complicated as they were in their family, you could arguably take your pick.

They were sitting on their beds facing one another. Lev's legs dangled; his grandfather's reached the floor.

Belonging, said Ferry, might be nothing more than a decision you make.

Water gushed into the tub from a rusty tap. It didn't flow; it gushed. When the tub was half full, Lev was stopped from getting in. Of several dozen baths in the dim light of the tiled room, only three others were in use. A woman in a light blue tunic was supervising. She checked the water level and temperature, helped people in and out without saying much, communicating with gestures, looks. She must have seen hundreds of people getting into the baths, all wanting to say the very same words. Her name badge said 'Irina', the surname shortened to an initial.

Lev climbed into the tub, hesitating because it was too hot – but this was a familiar game his mother played, always claiming that it wasn't. What was so hard to understand? If the person getting into the water said it was too hot, then it was too hot. The person outside the tub couldn't know. And though it was too hot, Lev sat down all the same; his trunks inflated, and he tried to tame them, but already felt the shudder spreading through his whole body, somewhere between pain and pleasure. He let out a groan.

Irina, who knew how to interpret, turned the tap to cold, and Lev gave her a grateful smile. So things were not the same here as at home.

When he'd sunk up to his chin, the tap was turned off. Irina shushed the murmuring coming from the other tubs. She poured the contents of a beaker into Lev's bath, and the scent of lavender, rosemary and something else rose from the water. Lev sank to the bottom. This was how a droplet must feel, dispersing in the Iza.

This sensation was new. His hands did not stop at his

fingertips, but continued into the air. The soles of his feet could feel every tile and join. His legs felt as if they would never tire again. Yet at the same time he was tired.

In the changing room, Lev stood in front of the mirror and found his face beautiful. He'd never thought that before. He turned his head from side to side. His skin was pale and freckled, all year round. His hair stuck to his scalp, and he ruffled it and laughed because it stuck up in all directions. He wrung out his trunks, hung them over a rail. Something drew him back to the mirror. He touched his cheeks and lips, imagined his hands were someone else's, and then ran a hand in one flowing movement down his chest and between his legs. His penis stood up. At once he let go, glanced around. Were those voices? But all was silent bar the dripping of his trunks. He picked up clothes and towel, clutched them all to him and went into a cubicle.

The blurred boundaries of his body stayed with him. They went with him to the room, where he lay on the bed reading, to dinner, where he smiled and said nothing; they were there when he met Ferry's questioning, knowing gaze, there when he sat on the bench that evening waiting for the squirrels. The squirrels came, one after another, until the lawn was filled with them, reddish brown, lighter underneath, with bushy tails and no fear of the spa guests. Everything was in motion, as if the ground itself was moving, the trees bending their branches low for the squirrels to leap on and off, restlessly driven by some inexplicable hurry which was perhaps joy.

Lonja arrived and passed him some hazelnuts. They knelt on the grass. More and more squirrels came, and Lev couldn't reach into the paper bag fast enough. He felt dizzy, her thigh against his, her side against his. When the bag was empty, Lonja took him in her arms, held him tight. He pressed his face to her neck, smelling soap and sweat, he could feel her collarbone. This was it. This must be what everyone talked about.

His grandfather didn't ask how it had been. He lay in bed reading, and every time he turned a page he sighed as if he liked the book a great deal, or not at all.

The light from the bedside lamp slanted across face, hand and book. Ferry only read short books; he didn't like long ones. He wasn't having some garrulous author stealing his time. This one was unusually thick, given his reading habits.

Lev undressed, placed his clothes neatly on a chair, slipped into his pyjamas, washed, brushed his teeth, went to the toilet, and although he was present in each action, he was also elsewhere. In bed he checked his timetable once more. Tomorrow he would take another herbal bath, tomorrow he would see Lonja again.

Why did the squirrels come at sunset?

How was Lonja's skin so soft?

Where on earth had she got a bag of nuts from?

Mr Radu arrived for breakfast without his wife. He feared she had caught a cold. Ferry reminded him that you had to dress warmly after the treatments. And take plenty of bed rest – lying down was generally crucial in life.

His wife knew that, Mr Radu countered, and it wasn't about lying down. He rather suspected it was the water temperature. They had started saving on everything here recently, he said, even the temperature of the water. Lev was surprised: he found the water wonderfully hot, too hot, even, and the very thought of another bath that afternoon made him feel warm. He spread honey energetically on his bread. Lonja threw him a conspiratorial smile across the table. Would he see her again that evening? Was she saying: same time, same place? You bring the nuts today? But he could come to no firm conclusion because then Lonja turned to the artist.

Without his wife's placatory presence, Mr Radu seemed much less inclined to let Lev's grandfather steer the conversation. Several times the two of them talked over one another; whatever the other said was to be contradicted. Was that masseuse called Anna or Anka? It must be Anna, her kneading was so timid, Mr Radu remarked. Should one towel dry after a bath or wrap oneself up still wet? A thorough towelling off was vital, said Ferry – perhaps that was the origin of his wife's cold. The older lady beside Silas made a movement, causing her crutches to fall to the floor. Mr Radu got up, hung them back on the chair. Taking advantage of this pause, she turned to Ferry and asked him about his work as a watch-glass maker, to which he responded unsuspectingly.

Returning to the room, Ferry tried to persuade his etui to dispense a cigarette, but the time was not yet up. Swearing, he put it away again. Lev was surprised at his grandfather. There was no reason for him to be at odds with Mr Radu. Both were long-time guests here, concerned about the quality of the food, the treatments, the accommodation. The reason had to lie elsewhere.

Lying in the bath that afternoon, Lev felt like a practised spa-goer. He knew where to put his clothes, when to enter the room, which was the right water level for climbing into the tub, when the herbs were added and the other guests' conversation fell silent. He knew that it was better to sit upright in the tub for a moment before standing, to dry yourself carefully, to drink a lot. All the preparations and all that came afterwards was in the service of time spent in the water. He got into the (always slightly too hot) bath, Irina cast an amused glance at him, then ran some cold water. He pressed his trunks down and sank up to his chin. Now that thing could approach that for the rest of the day went on reaching out to him from afar.

Lonja's beauty, he realised in the bath, wasn't the kind that struck you right away. She was as mysterious as those river pebbles that revealed their colours only when wet. When he closed his eyes then eyes, nose, mouth combined to form this one face. What mattered was not just the exact position of features, but the spaces between.

When Irina returned (always slightly too soon), he pushed his daydreams and musings aside. It was some time before he could give his body the order to move.

'Irina, where does a person get hazelnuts here?'

Window and balcony door were open. Ferry had piled up his pillows and was lying propped on them so his gastric juices wouldn't rise. Lunch had been lavish, soup and meatloaf, with torte for dessert, a Russian Elegante layered with cream.

Lev copied his grandfather at first, then pushed his pillows down to his feet. His body felt large, so large it scarcely seemed to fit on the mattress.

'Is it time now?'

'Time for what?'

'For the story about why you're Austrian.'

At first it looked as if Ferry had no desire to answer; then Lev realised he was searching for the right beginning.

In his life, said Ferry, he had been several things. He'd been launched into this century as an Austrian and, without moving from the spot geographically, he'd become Romanian, then Hungarian, and finally, though his passport again said he was Romanian, he'd decided that he would remain Austrian.

To Lev, whose citizenship and passport had never changed, that seemed monstrous.

Until nineteen-nineteen, Transylvania and the Maramureş had belonged to Austria-Hungary, Ferry explained, then to the Kingdom of Romania. Twenty years later it was passed back to Hungary and, four years on, to Romania again. All this, as Lev could well imagine, had been tiresome. Now he was deciding for himself. Why should his own decision be any worse than those made by some people in some capital city or other?

Lev nodded. No less was expected of him.

'But one day,' said Ferry, 'because we've made too little effort, or too much, it will be over for us. We have been weighed in the balance and found wanting.'

Lev looked questioningly at his grandfather, but Ferry didn't notice. He was lying on the bed, pillows under his back, hands by his sides – like a pharaoh, thought Lev.

'Radu knows it, he's already got the victor's sense of superiority. He just has to wait, and we'll leave of our own free will, as soon as we can, we'll go. There'll be no stopping it.'

What was Lev?

He was the rooms, the yard, the village street, the valley, the hills, the river. Spider silk, vine tendrils, grass paths and river pebbles. The lawn, the loggias that wrapped around the houses, the give of the stairs, the sound of the lanes, the river – all this extended into him; he was all of it. And he could see it clearly now, because for the first time it was absent.

He knew nothing of going away. Only of absences.

Lis had been nineteen when she met his father; the state had sent them both to work at bringing in the harvest. He was a widower, looking for a mother for the three children from his first marriage. Despite resistance from Ferry and Bunica, the pair married, and Lev was their only child together. He had very few memories of his father, who had died in a landslip when Lev was five years old. The little he did remember, he recalled over and over: his father's hands, the smell of his grey sheepskin waistcoat, his footsteps in the hall. And sometimes, when Lev came into the house, he felt his father was waiting for him.

His mother said that Dorin and Bredica were like him, with their green eyes, their equanimity and pride. She told him about her late father-in-law, too. He had understood the love between them, and was the only one who hadn't minded that they weren't the same nationality.

Lev had no maternal grandmother.

No paternal grandfather.

He had no father.

And the other person missing was Ferry.

In all these years, he'd hardly visited.

After dinner, as Lev was leaving the dining room with his grandfather, someone pulled him aside. It took a moment to recognise Irina without her tunic.

'Here,' she said, giving him a bag. 'You wanted nuts, yes?'

In place of an answer, he threw his arms around her.

Bag in hand, he ran after his grandfather.

Lev and Ferry arrived just as the sun was getting tangled in the plane trees. It poured liquid orange over the branches, flooded the lawn with light that was almost horizontal. Lonja's silhouette seemed blurred. As the light took possession of her, the shadows gathered, and while squirrels went on appearing until the grass was swarming with them, for a moment the sun seemed to dissolve Lonja's figure, as if her body might vanish with the light.

They sat on a bench and fed the squirrels. Ferry chatted to Lonja, and although Lev would have liked to be alone with her, he didn't mind that his grandfather had come too. This way he could look at her without having to talk. Later, he was astonished to hear Ferry say that this woman harboured a great sadness.

The cinema filled up and the red curtains swung aside. Lev followed the riders, the clouds, the birds of passage, and a father's attempt to quiet his child's crying by promising 'youth without old age and life without death'. He watched the son go out into the world to look for those things when the father couldn't keep his promise – but actually all he saw was Lonja, sitting diagonally in front of him.

During dinner the sisters had argued again, their muted

voices growing so loud that the others at the table could no longer ignore them. She would not collude in this sneaking around any longer, Lonja's sister cried, and left the dining hall before the main course was over. Lonja went on eating with a show of composure, avoiding looking up, even when Ferry laid a hand on hers – placatory, comforting, and questioning, too. Lev waited for her outside the dining hall, but she sent him away.

He didn't understand her troubles, she said.

The screen was a riot of colours, music and voices, but as they met Lev's eyes and ears they were all extinguished, like a burning match falling into water. If only he knew what was wrong.

When the son reached the Kingdom of Eternal Youth and was given three tasks, someone entered Lonja's row and sat in the vacant seat beside her. First the 'corn ear of goodness' and the 'apple of truth' had to be found; they were hidden in the Kingdom of Lies, for liars scorned the truth. The third task was to track down the missing key to a book. He who found it was permitted to read the book and remain. While the hero carried out his quest, married the king's daughter and failed to notice the passing of time (how could he, since years were days to him), Ferry fell asleep. Lev watched Lonja's head tilt towards the artist's, and he thought that it must be a lie, a lie, a lie.

Only two more days.

He would get up, have breakfast, bathe twice more.

Everything had run backwards, shrunk, and their huge stretch of time was now mercilessly shortening. Ferry seemed untroubled by this; he would return. Would Lev return, too?

And if he did, would everything be as it was now? Like a house whose door you could push open and find everything just as you'd left it. The brightly lit dining room would be there, the room with two beds, the bathing hall, the smell of chlorine and herbs, Irina, the squirrels. The table company would be there, meeting three times a day for meals – only the artist would be missing, Lev wished him away. How to bid Lonja farewell? What should he say? In his fantasy, they would meet again, year after year, until he learned how to tell a woman what his feelings were.

Lev wanted to ask Lonja for her address. Ferry said he shouldn't deceive himself: people became friendly on a health cure, but this was just an interlude, and as such finite. On a certain day it would be over. Eventually, and Ferry was convinced of this, there would be a woman in Lev's life whom he wasn't to let go. Someone worth waiting for, worth any hazard, any length of time.

After lunch, Lev's timetable prescribed a walk. He decided to stick to it; in these last two days he would do everything written on the light blue slip, now dog-eared and crumpled in his pocket. At home there would be no such slip, and Lev marvelled at how little thought he'd given to his family, to his village, and even the mountains and hills whose absence he had felt so keenly at the start.

He took the path along the colonnade, past the coffeehouse and the former imperial villa, through the park with its plane trees, until he reached a building that had to be the bottling plant for the curative waters.

He considered taking some back for his mother but dismissed the idea at once. The water tasted disgusting, and he only choked it down to avoid showing weakness in front of Irina. He caught sight of Lonja and Silas behind the boundary fence. They were arguing. Not an argument with words, the words didn't matter; it was mainly their bodies doing the arguing. Lonja turned her back on Silas, walked a few paces, then returned. Silas raised his hands, appeasing, reassuring, then grabbed her arm and didn't let go even when she tried to free herself. Lev ran along the barrier, shaking the fence. Stop it, he called out, or did he just think the words? He felt sick. He wasn't someone looking for an entrance; he was shut in. There was no escape for him.

He bent, picked up a stone and threw it over the fence. The pair spotted Lev, turned away, and were lost from view. Finally, the fence became low enough to climb over. He snagged his trousers, hardly noticed that he was bleeding, scrambled to his feet. When he reached the place where the two had disappeared, he called Lonja's name. Several buildings, warehouses with water tanks, forklifts, pallets of canisters, cardboard. A man in overalls approached and asked what he was doing here. Lev stammered something about a couple, an argument. The man seemed undecided, eying Lev and his bleeding leg. Then they heard the scream.

The man took off, Lev followed, and they ran between two buildings, past a tank and along a path that curved towards an open area, the man quickening his pace and then stopping so abruptly that Lev crashed into him. They were in a field of unmown grass, inset with deep, round concrete basins. Puddles of water, scattered rubbish, fallen leaves. Lev went to step out from behind the man, but the man made him promise to stay where he was, not to move.

'Stai aşa, băiete!'

Silas was crouching by a basin in a strange posture, face turned towards the ground. This – he never meant for this to happen.

The workman looked down into the basin and both hands went to his mouth. Lev wanted to step up to the edge, too, but something was rooting him to the spot, preventing him from going any further.

His legs. He couldn't move his legs.

Renebuëġen,
guldiwerzuëġen,
äm Hemmel äs e selij Mån,
diër de Ren verdreiwe kån.

One

Softness. Something warm.

Far-off voices.

A faint pulse behind his brow, the size of a pinhead.

Light slanting in from one side.

Just a dream?

Footsteps approached. A song. A voice like a young girl's. But wasn't that his mother?

Light, noises, everything sank into him and he was defenceless. Weariness made everything the same, blurring thoughts, faces. Outside it was getting light.

His father came into the room wearing a waistcoat of grey, curly lamb's wool; a familiar, sour smell. Lev tried to sit up but his father pressed him back down, gently, firmly. His hands were warm.

Lev knew that he wanted to say goodbye. He was gripped by an inexplicable fear; he had to get out of bed, put his clothes on, go with his father – when would he be old enough to go? To cut wood, plant trees, repair hiking paths. Wait another year, his father said when he asked. Another year. And when that was up, he put him off again. Everything kept going further away instead of coming closer. Lev wanted to tell him he was old enough now, and if not now, then next year, but his tongue was heavy and dry in his mouth.

He reached for his father's hand.

'Go back to sleep,' his father said. 'I'll be home again soon.'

Lev nodded, looked at him. Tried to put everything into that look. Love. Determination. Longing. His father always brought something back for him and his brothers and sister: interestingly shaped stones, animal bones, root wood. Lev waited for his return, and each time it seemed to be the other way round, as if his father was waiting for him, filled with curiosity to see who Lev had become while he was away.

Now Lis was in the room as well.

'It's started raining,' she said.

Lev was still holding his father's hand.

'Lev?'

'Mm-hm.'

'You can let go now.'

ACKNOWLEDGEMENTS

My thanks to the Deutscher Literaturfonds for the generous grant. To the Stadt Schwäbisch Hall and the Staatliche Akademie Comburg, the Otto-Ubbelohde-Stiftung and Verein Zwei Raben, Literatur in Oberhessen for the periods of silence and writing.

To Andreas Thies, Rico Müller-Schmitt, Julia Knapp, Daniel Meurer, and Renate and Helmut Wolff for early readings and encouragement.

To Maria Cristina Tangorra, Heinrich Haltrich, Günter Wolff, Traute and Sissy Habicher, Ursula Stefanovici, Bernd Lögler, Hartwig Ochsenfeld, and Björn and Flore Reinhardt for their memories and inspiration. Thank you for trusting me!

To Dr. Sigrid Haldenwang, Dr. Norina Procopan, Dr. András Balogh, Prof. Dr. Hans-Jürgen Schrader, Damaschin Pop-Buia, Renate Schmidgall, Angelika Meltzer, Luminița Cioabă, Vasilena Beuca, Nicolae Bucurici, Ada Andrea Zsigmond, Dieter David and Karina Korecky for the sayings and translations.

To Stefanie Schwab und Andreas Heizler from Jägerhofsäge Heizler, Klaus Echle from the Freiburg Forestry Office, Manuel Karopka from the Forstliche Versuchs- und Forschungsanstalt

Baden-Württemberg and the forester Sophie Karopka for research and advice.

And to my publisher Klett-Cotta Verlag and the Copywrite agency, in particular my editor Corinna Kroker and my agent Caterina Schäfer. Would Lev and Kato's world even exist without you?

I am grateful to Monique Charlesworth, who has given my books a home in England, and my translator, Ruth Martin. My thanks to you both for the bond we share, from snow globes to sycamore propellers.

QUOTATIONS

• • • • •

Nine

It was, and it was not.

Traditional opening to Roma folktales

Eight

I am the sign of the journey. Unmoving.

From the poem *Delfiny* by Adam Zagajewski

Seven

Pictures of You

Song title by The Cure

Six

A wolf and a lamb were driven by thirst to a river. The wolf stood upstream, the lamb downstream. On a pretext, the wolf began an argument. 'Why,' he asked, 'have you muddied the water I am drinking?'

Retelling of the Aesop fable 'The Wolf and the Lamb', in the Ruthenian dialect of the Ruscova Valley

Five

Through the forests I will go
And see my fill of leafgreen
In the valleys and on the mountain

Lyrics by Maria Tănase, *Doină din Maramureş*

Four

Here you have nothing, hold onto it.

Hungarian saying

Three

Then all the birds and wild animals came, and the cat chose the most beautiful, brightly coloured feathers and made of them a cloak that glittered and shone like the starry sky, and gave it to the boy.

The Feather King, Transylvanian folk tale

Two

This is the inscription that was written: mene, mene, tekel, parsin. Here is what these words mean: *Mene*: God has numbered the days of your reign and brought it to an end. *Tekel*: You have been weighed on the scales and found wanting. *Peres*: Your kingdom is divided and given to the Medes and Persians.

Book of Daniel 5:25-28, The Holy Bible, New International Version

One

Rainbow
Golden glow
In heaven there's a blessed man
Who can drive away the rain

Transylvanian children's rhyme, Sighişoara dialect

REFERENCES AND ACKNOWLEDGEMENTS

• • • • •

Ausländer, Rose: 'Noch bist du da', in: *Gesammelte Werke*, Helmut Braun. vol. V: *Ich höre das Herz des Oleanders. Gedichte 1977–1979*, © 1984. Quotation by permission of S. Fischer Verlag GmbH, Frankfurt am Main.

'Der Federkönig', in: *Sächsische Volksmärchen aus Siebenbürgen*, ed. Dieter Roth. Technical editor Constanța Vulcănescu. Illustrated by Helmut Arz and Kathrin Hienz. Jugendverlag, Bucharest, 1967

'Die Nebelfrauen', in: *Zipser Volkserzählungen aus der Maramuresch, der Südbukowina und dem Nösner Land*, ed. Claus Stephani. Kriterion Verlag, Bucharest, 1981

'Kinderreim bei Regenbogen', in: *E Liedchen hälft ängden. Alte und neue Lieder aus Siebenbürgen*, ed. Angelika Meltzer and Rosemarie Chrestels. Verlag Haus der Heimat, Nuremberg, 2020.

Lenau, Nikolaus: 'Himmelstrauer', in: *Die schönsten Gedichte von Nikolaus Lenau. Ausgewählt von Silvia Sager. Mit einem Nachwort von Berthold Auerbach.* Diogenes Verlag AG, Zurich, 2002.

Tănase, Maria: 'Doină din Maramuresch'. Album: *Vol 2. Casa de discuri,* Electrecord s. a. Bucharest, recorded between 1953 and 1961, released 2007.

The Cure: '*Pictures of you*'. Album: *Disintegration.* Fiction Records, London, 1989.

The Holy Bible, New International Version ®, NIV® Copyright © 1973, 1978, 1984, 2011 by Biblica, Inc.®, accessed online at https://www.biblegateway.com/versions/New-International-Version-NIV-Bible

Zagajewski, Adam: 'Delfiny', in: *Anteny.* Verlag a5, Krakow, 2005. Quotation by kind permission of Maja Zagajewska, Verlag a5 and Farrar, Straus & Giroux, LLC.

TRANSLATOR'S NOTE

• • • • •

In German, this book contains a few key words that can't be translated the same way every time, and so I am grateful to have the space here to pass these on to readers of the English edition. The first two, *Herkunft* and *Zukunft,* have a kind of symmetry and an etymological link that doesn't exist in any of their English counterparts. A person's *Herkunft* is their origin, their social, national and cultural roots. Where they come from, and when. *Zukunft* is the future – though in fact the symmetry here is deceptive. It doesn't mean where someone is actively going to, but what is coming towards them, what lies in store. The novel travels backwards into Lev and Kato's past, showing us what has shaped them, and asks the life-changing question of whether to stay behind or set out into the unknown – so the poles that these terms represent underpin the whole narrative. In English, I have added to the tissue of their meaning each time they appear, teasing out what German readers will take from the two words in different contexts. The effect is necessarily a more subtle one, but I don't believe that anything is lost here: rather, translation is an opportunity to view these everyday words with fresh eyes, and articulate resonances that might only register on a subconscious level with readers of the original.

A related term that lies somewhere between these poles is *Ankunft*: arrival. Lev's arrival in Zurich at the start of the novel is not the end of the story, but a staging post in his and Kato's journey into an as yet unwritten future. The shape of the word ties it into the journey from *Herkunft* to *Zukunft*: it is made from the same building blocks of prefix + *kunft*, an alternative form of *kommen*, which simply means *to come*. And this root-word is the same one Kato uses on the postcard to Lev that spurs him into action and brings them back together: 'When are you coming?'

Perhaps the most complex word in the book is the verb *aufbrechen*, and its related noun *Aufbruch*. Often, it simply means to set off, though with a particular sense of suddenness and purpose, and comes from the same idea as the English 'decamp': to break down your tents and move on. *Aufbrechen* looks ahead, to where someone is going, and so I have avoided the possible translation 'leave', which looks back at what is left behind. The other meanings of *aufbrechen*, which always echo within it, are to do with breaking things open (a lock, a door), rooting up the earth, or opening up like a flower or a wound. And of course, no English word reflects this exact constellation. Again, my translations of *aufbrechen* are a collection of terms that add up to a more expansive meaning, though readers won't see the repetition present in the German. I have translated the verb most often as 'set off' or 'set out', with a hint of new beginnings where it appears as a noun – because *Aufbruch* can mean departure, but also a spiritual awakening or uprising. 'Du willst aufbrechen?' Kato asks Lev in Zurich. 'Ready to go?' That 'go' is the starting pistol for an adventure;

they don't yet know where they are going, just somewhere new, to meet whatever future is coming towards them.

Ruth Martin